WHEN THE TIDE TURNS

BOOK THREE
GRAVE ENCOUNTER SERIES

Turn the Tide: To reverse the course of events

A 1940's Romance

KAY CHANDLER

This is a work of fiction. Characters, places and incidents are the products of the author's imagination or are used fictitiously.

Cover Design by Chase Chandler

DEDICATED TO MURRAY & LOTTIE

It seems only fitting that I dedicate this particular book to the memory of my precious mother and dad, Murray and Lottie McCall.

In the late 1950's they received a call from the Child Welfare Department asking if they could foster three siblings, ages 6, 5 and 4, who had no place to go. After keeping the children for ten months and learning to love them as their own, my parents tried to adopt them.

There was a hearing, and even though the biological parents showed up and asked the judge to allow my parents to keep them, they were denied. The reason: the parents lived in the same county and could try to take them back at a later date. They were told the children would be likely split up and put up for adoption. Broken-hearted, my parents exhausted every avenue. Mother made an appointment with the Governor of the State of Alabama, pleading their case, to no avail.

Roy Gene, Betty Joyce and Billy Ray Quattlebaum, if you're out there, I can assure you that Aunt Lottie and Uncle Murray, as you called them, never gave up hope that one day they'd hear from you. Please know that you were very much loved and wanted.

Just as little Alexandra in this novel was loved and wanted.

Chapter One

Foggy Bottom, Alabama
February, 1940

"I know how you hate deceit, Mack, but honestly, what good could come from telling a child her father is an unknown rapist?" Dabney Foxworthy, nursemaid to Parson Mack Pruitt's ten-year-old granddaughter, reached across the table and gently placed her hand on her employer's arm.

"Unknown? Somehow, Dabs, I've always had the feeling he was unknown to me, but not necessarily unknown to you. However, it's probably best I don't know. I'm afraid of what I'd do to the scumbag."

Her face flushed hot when his eyes met hers. Maybe it was because of the strong desire to stand, walk around the table and embrace him in her arms. Not in a romantic way, but the way a loving mother comforts a hurting child. She swallowed hard. What would she know about a mother's love? Alexandra wasn't her child, and all the pretending wouldn't make it so. Dabney would never have imagined it possible to become so attached to someone else's child. Yet, neither could she have fathomed that she'd still be living in the Pruitt household ten years after little Alexandra was born. With Zann's death following the baby's birth and the parson's mentally incapacitated wife locked away at Bryce's Insane Asylum, Dabney had continued to live with the Reverend, serving as the maid and surrogate mother to Alexandra. But a lot of things happened in the past decade she could never have imagined. The phone shattered her thoughts. "Shall I answer it, Mack?"

He shrugged, dismissively. "No, thanks, I'll take it." He lifted from his chair and walked into the hall. "Parson Pruitt's residence."

Calling the preacher by his first name came natural, now; yet, when he first suggested she drop the Parson title, Dabney couldn't seem to call him anything other than, "Hey you." It didn't seem proper to address her employer in such a familiar manner. But through the years, he'd become much more than just her employer. Not that she could verbalize, even to herself, exactly what type relationship they shared. She only knew there was nothing in the world she wouldn't do for the man. Legal or moral, that is. She'd long ago given up the notion of marriage, but if she ever did find someone, he'd have to be kind, considerate and loving . . . like Mack. And the odds of finding such a man seemed nil. Mack Pruitt was one-of-a-kind.

Dabney sensed from the one-sided phone conversation that it was a call from the Asylum in Tuscaloosa. She hoped the doctor simply wanted to give Mack a positive progress report on Mrs. Pruitt's condition. Though it had been ten years of ups and downs with back and forth trips from the hospital, the dedicated husband never gave up hope that with proper care and medication, his mentally ill wife would one day be well again.

His somber expression when he lumbered back into the kitchen told her the news was not good. Without a word, he opened the screen door leading to the porch, and from the window, Dabney could see him leaning against the railing, his shoulders drooped. The past year had taken its toll on him. His appetite had waned and Dabney could hear him pacing the floor at night. She'd altered the waist of his slacks until the belt loops were practically touching. Swallowing the pain in her throat, she watched his thin body convulse in steady sobs. If he continued losing weight, he'd be nothing but skin and bone. She glanced at the clock above the stove when the front door slammed. *Three-fifteen, already?* Where had the time gone?

Alexandra came tripping into the house, yelling, "Dabs? Where are you, Dabs?"

"In the kitchen, hon. How was your day?"

"Good. No, I take that back. It was better than good. It was really, really swell!" She returned Dabney's hug, and then waving an envelope in the air, said, "Guess what? I got my report card today and I made all A's. Where's Daddy Mack? I want to show him."

"That's wonderful, sweetheart. I'm so proud of you. But I

have an idea. Why don't you wait until supper, and we'll turn your Daddy Mack's plate upside down, and when he flips it over, he'll see that excellent report card. It'll be a fun surprise." Dabney silently praised herself for quick thinking.

Alexandra jumped up and down with her hands clasped together. "That's a super-duper idea, Dabs." She grabbed two oatmeal cookies from the pie safe.

"Have a seat at the table, dear, and I'll pour you a glass of milk to go with them."

The parson ambled into the house and seeing his granddaughter, feigned a smile. Alexandra ran and threw her arms around his waist. "Daddy Mack, I have a surprise but you can't see it until suppertime. It's a great surprise. Right, Dabs?"

"Absolutely. But we won't give it away, yet. If you've finished with your snack, please go pull off your good school clothes and put on your jeans."

Mack managed to hold the smile, though his jaws ached from forcing the uncooperative facial muscles to respond. He patted his granddaughter's head. "Sounds good, Ladybug." He abruptly left the room and headed toward the parlor.

Alexandra grabbed two more cookies from the pie safe. "Dabs, can I go catch tadpoles after I change clothes?"

"*May* I . . ."

"Sorry. May I?"

"Yes, but make sure you're home before dark."

4

Dabney puttered around the kitchen, hoping Mack would mention the phone call. Not that it was any of her business, but in the past he'd been so open and willing to share his thoughts. For the past few weeks, however, he seemed to be sinking into a deep depression. Perhaps if he could express what he was feeling, it wouldn't seem so overwhelming. She carried him a cup of hot coffee, sat it on the table beside his chair and reluctantly turned to walk out.

"Wait, Dabney." He patted the couch cushion beside him, urging her to take a seat. "Where's Alexandra?"

"She just ran out of the house on the way to the pond. Shall I call her back?"

"No. I don't want her to hear what I have to say." He twisted his hands together, then pulled on each finger, popping them one by one with a swift jerk.

Dabney learned long ago to recognize the nervous habit as a precursor to unpleasant news.

"The phone call was from the hospital."

"I figured as much." Not wanting to press him, she waited, giving him ample time to get his thoughts together.

He caught his lower lip between his teeth. "Dabney, my Dora won't be coming back. Ever."

"You don't know that, Mack. Maybe after a few more treatments—"

Not letting her finish, he shook his head. "But it's true."

Taking a cue from the pain in his eyes, she asked the question

5

he seemed to be waiting for. "So what did the doctor suggest?"

"It felt more like a command than a suggestion. I suppose working in such a horrible environment would tend to make one callous, but the ruthless doctor's cold words keep playing in my head like a broken phonograph record. He said, 'Parson, it's time to put her out of your mind.' Then he snickered and said, 'It's a fact you're no longer on *her* mind. Your wife is hopelessly insane. She doesn't remember you and never will, so the best thing you can do is to get on with your life.'"

"Surely, you misunderstood. Maybe he blew his nose and it only sounded as if he snickered. Or it could've been static in the connection."

"I promise you, I heard what I heard." Mack reached for the coffee cup and took a sip. "You know what I told him?"

The lump in her throat prevented her from answering.

"I told him if he couldn't help her, I'd bring her home and I'd take care of her myself."

Dabney clasped her hands together in her lap to hide the trembling. "So, is that what you plan to do?"

"Unfortunately, no. It seems according to the law, I no longer have a say-so in what happens to my wife. I never should've let them take her away. Now, they won't release her. It was bad enough six years ago when I learned they sterilized her without my permission. There was no call for that. It was cruel. She's not an animal, and it's not as if we—"

His face reddened slightly. "Forgive me. Dabney. I have no

right to talk to you about such a private, sensitive subject." He stroked his chin with his hand. "I'm obviously having trouble thinking straight. But for the life of me, I can't believe the man would have the gall to sit up there in his white coat, behind his big fine desk and tell me what to do, when he has no idea the struggles I'm dealing with. He's Dora's doctor, for crying out loud—not mine, and he doesn't even have a clue what to do for her. 'Get on with your life.' That's what he said. 'Get on with your life.' That's easy for him to say. *What* life?"

His moist eyes pleaded for help, but Dabney had none to give. "I'm so sorry, Mack."

He stood and walked over to the fireplace with his back to her. "Insane," he mumbled.

"I beg your pardon?" The peculiar look on his face when he whirled around, caused chills to run up her spine.

"Insane. There, I said it. My wife is insane."

She walked over and stood beside him. "She's sick, Mack, but sick people get well."

"No. You know better and so do I. The doctor said I was afraid of admitting the truth. Maybe he's right. I've called it stress, exhaustion, nerves—anything but insanity, because the truth hurts." His eyes welled with tears.

Her instinct told her to take him in her arms and let him know it was okay to cry, but she'd learned long ago not to trust her instincts. "Mack, he was wrong. It wasn't fear, but love that kept you from wanting to admit it. I know how much you love her."

7

His face distorted. "Do you, Dabney? Do you really know, because I'm not too sure anymore if its love or pity I feel for Dora. I *did* love her. Once. But it's difficult sometimes for me to distinguish the Dora I married from the Dora who now looks at me with terrifying eyes. For ten years, she's been a stranger to me. I made a vow 'til death do us part, and yet now we're parted by something far worse than death. Forgive me for wallowing in pity, when Dora is the one to be pitied. No human should endure the kind of treatment forced upon her at that horrid hospital. The inmates are treated like wild animals. Who wouldn't go crazy in a place like that?" He grimaced and rubbed his chest as if doing so could soothe a broken heart.

A peculiar curiosity stirred within her when his eyes focused on her mouth, causing her to quickly swipe her lips with the back of her hand, assuming she had something on her face. His gaze trailed down, then up, and back down again, as if searching her intently from head to toe. Dabney quickly dismissed the absurd thoughts scrambling for a place to rest. He was a preacher, for crying out loud, and a married one at that. "Why don't you lay down before supper. You look exhausted."

"I think I will. But I know as soon as I close my eyes, the dream will return."

"A nightmare?"

"Of the worse kind. Every night I dream I'm swimming in dark, murky waters, fighting frantically to stay afloat to keep from drowning—yet the shore is nowhere in sight. I'm out there all alone. Then a lifeboat comes close, and I can see two hands reaching down to help me. I want desperately to reach up and grab them . . . but for some unknown reason, just as our fingers are within an inch of touching, the boat invariably drifts a little further away and we're unable to connect." His voice cracked. "If only the boat would come close enough for me to grasp those helping hands, but I always wake up and realize nothing will ever change. Ever. We'll never touch. So I get up and walk the floor to keep from going back to sleep and reliving the same terrifying nightmare."

"Mack, I'm certainly not a dream interpreter, but do you suppose the dream represents a subconscious feeling you have that Mrs. Pruitt is reaching out to you for help and you're understandably distraught, because regardless of how hard you keep trying to reach her, she keeps drifting away?"

"No."

The coldness in his blunt answer caught her by surprise. "As I said, I'm no dream interpreter. It was just a thought."

"Dabney, I can see the hands and they don't belong to my wife. I know those hands. I see them daily, preparing my meals, washing my clothes, making my bed, carrying for my grandchild."

A lump formed in her throat. "It's just a dream, Mack."

He had a faraway look in his eyes. "Yes. A dream." His Adam's apple bobbed. "Dabney . . . if things had been different, do you suppose . . . ?"

He ran his hands through his thick brown hair.

9

"But things aren't different, Mack. They are what they are, so who am I to speculate about something I have no way of knowing?"

He shrugged. "You're right. I was just rambling. Tired, I guess. Call me when supper's ready. I think I'll go lay down for a few minutes."

Mack Pruitt kicked off his shoes and stretched out on the bed, but with so much conflict stirring inside, he couldn't rest. He recalled the countless sermons he'd preached, declaring that temptations only became sin when acted upon. Now, he wasn't so sure. If the thought wasn't sinful, why did he carry such guilt? He shuddered at how uncomfortably close he'd come lately into turning a thought into an action.

He got up, reached on the top shelf in the closet and pulled down a hat box that held Dora's keepsakes. It felt somewhat sneaky going through her personal belongings, but by sifting through the paraphernalia hidden away in that large pink box, he might somehow recapture the good times that were slowly fading from his memory. He had to hold on, somehow. He'd made a vow to God, a vow he couldn't break. Nineteen years of a happy marriage came to a screeching halt the day they buried their eighteen-year-old daughter. A part of Dora died along with Zann that day. He pulled out a small snapshot made on their wedding day. The young couple in the picture looked happy enough. Could that really be him, grinning from ear to ear, with his arm around a woman he could barely remember? The beautiful young woman in the photo looked nothing like the wild-eyed, frightened creature locked away at Bryce's.

Mack clinched his eyes tightly and lifted up a prayer. *Oh, Lord, please help me. I need my wife and I need her well. This situation at home is becoming too much to bear. I don't like these thoughts I'm having. Deliver me, Father from these vain imaginations.*

Piece by piece, he lifted the contents from the hat box. There were old newspaper clippings of their wedding, souvenirs from their vacation to Warm Springs, a small velvet bag with a lock of their deceased daughter's curls, saved from her first haircut. But it was his darling daughter's school pictures that brought a rush of tears to his eyes. "Why, Lord? Why my sweet Zann? Why not me?"

Chapter Two

Oliver Weinberger never wanted to be in politics, but then he was never asked what he wanted. And being the dutiful son he was brainwashed to be, he always did exactly as told. Reluctantly, but always without a whimper. His illustrious father had been a Senator, and before him, his father, and his father before him. From the day he was born, Oliver was groomed to take the generational torch.

He understood too well the disappointment he brought upon his doting mother, Lula, when he refused to run for the seat. But must he spend the remainder of his life trying to make up for it? Was there nothing he could do to make her understand he wasn't cut out of the same cloth as his bigger-than-life father? Oliver had no aspirations to walk in the Senator's footsteps. He longed to make a difference in the lives of others—to somehow believe that his own life counted for something. His secret desire had been to finish law school, set up practice in a place where no one knew him as Senator Weinberger's son, and to take on pro-bono cases. However, to find a town where the Weinberger name was unknown would take him half-way around the United States, and with his mother's heart condition, there was no way he could venture very far from Goat Hill.

Oliver spent his last months in school researching small towns close enough to his domineering mother that he'd be able to reach her in case of an emergency, yet far enough away that he didn't feel smothered by her daily overbearing demands on his life. But the day he finished law school, he came home to discover that she'd remodeled the house and built an elaborate law office with an outside entrance, complete with a shingle above the door.

When he walked in and viewed it for the first time, his mother clasped her hands under her chin and gushed, "I could hardly wait for you to see your surprise, Oliver. Isn't it a lovely work place?" A sick feeling swept over him. It was Lula Weinberger's way of insuring that her precious son would never be out of arm's reach. And as always, Oliver would cower to her demands.

He glared at the furniture in the far corner and stuttered as he pointed. "Please tell me that's a joke, Mother. A purple velvet desk chair?" He squinted his eyes and blinked repeatedly, in hopes the garish image would disappear.

"Oh, hon, I know you've never been fond of the color purple, but I was fortunate to be able to employ Pierre from Designs for Discriminating Tastes as our decorator. He's highly sought, you know, and it can often take as long as a year to get him."

"You paid someone to sell you . . . *that*?"

"But sweetheart, it isn't just a desk chair."

Oliver sucked in a heavy breath of air and let it out slowly. "Mother, I think you mean it's *not even* a desk chair."

"Sit in it, dear. Lean back, close your eyes and relax and I'm sure you'll decide differently. Pierre has made a comprehensive study of colors. He says shades of purple are known to have a psychological effect on the mind, allowing one to concentrate and become much more productive than, say, someone who is surrounded by the color orange. According to Pierre, orange tends to exaggerate flightiness in an individual with those particular tendencies. I found it fascinating to discover how the various colors effect our moods and shape our paths."

He placed his arm around her shoulder. "I know you meant well, Mother, and I'm sorry to disappoint, but the overstuffed chair has to go. We'll return it tomorrow. I'll replace it with a brown leather swivel chair. I'm sure I can find what I'm looking for at Johnson's Furniture."

"Silly boy, Designs for Discriminating Tastes is a high-end studio and even if I were interested in returning it—which I'm not—they don't give refunds. I'll admit, I too, was taken aback at first glance, but after a long consultation, Pierre convinced me it's the perfect fit for your office."

"Mother, in spite of what that Pierre fellow says about the psychological effects, the funny, fuzzy chair will be history after today. If I'm less productive sitting in a nice, brown leather chair, then so be it."

"Oliver Kipling Weinberger, you're being childish. The chair is staying right where it is, and that's final. I paid too much money to consider replacing it with a common chair."

Why argue. When Lula Weinberger made up her mind, a team of wild horses couldn't sway her. He shook his head and winced. *Purple velvet?*

"I'm not shocked at your reaction, dear. I expected as much, but there's no expense I would spare, if it helps you become the man your father was. What a brilliant man. When I filled out the questionnaire and completed the interview, I mentioned to Pierre that you sometimes have a tendency to daydream and lose sight of reality. That's when he took me to the back of the showroom and pointed out this one-of-a kind chair. He says it was specifically designed for another client who has trouble staying focused, but the poor man died before it was delivered."

"I almost had the same reaction when I saw it."

"Your humor is ill-placed, Oliver."

"Sorry, but let me get this straight. You filled out a questionnaire and were interviewed before you were allowed to purchase a chair? Why?"

"Pierre is dedicated to putting the right furniture with the right client. There was a whole section I had to fill out on your habits and quirks. Then, afterward, he spent over three hours going over my answers and asking questions."

Gotta stay calm. Can't kill her. She's my mama. "What else

15

did you tell him, Mother?" Oliver's voice squeaked, as if he were going through puberty all over again.

"It was a rather lengthy questionnaire. Let me think." She placed her index finger against her cheek. "Oh, yes, he was fascinated when I told him about that ridiculous notion you had once, when you decided money meant nothing to you. I believe your exact words were, 'I'm not materialistic.' Remember, darling? You were very dogmatic in declaring that your clients would all be pro-hobos." Her lips parted and she let out a faint tee-hee.

"Pro bono, Mother. Not pro hobo."

"Hobo, bono, what's the difference? It means vagrants who expect you to represent them without pay, doesn't it? I had to bite my tongue to keep from expressing my opinion back then, but I won't hesitate to tell you, now that you've come to your senses, that cockeyed idea of yours frightened me."

"Perhaps you've forgotten, Mother, dear, but if I remember correctly, you were quite verbal at the time. You were ready to throw me on the first boat sailing to Siam. There was no guessing where you stood on the issue. No guessing at all."

"Really? Maybe I did forget. But you'll have to admit, it's not like me to interfere. I normally try to stay out of your business and let you make your own decisions. I'm just glad you finally came to your senses. Your father was a borderline genius, you know, and never had trouble staying focused on the things that were important. It's a shame you couldn't have inherited more of his traits, but I fear you take after that fickle mother of his." She clicked her tongue a couple of times, the way she always did, when speaking of her late mother-in-law. "I declare, I've never known a more unpredictable individual. Not that she was unscrupulous, mind you, but she didn't seem to have a grasp of the things that were important in life. How J.D. came out with such a head on his shoulders is nothing short of a miracle."

Oliver placed his arm over her shoulder and feigned a look of pity. "It *is* unfortunate, indeed, that I took after Grandmother and not Father. Do you suppose it could be the purple versus orange phenomenon? After all, Father ate grapes and I suck oranges. Of course! That's it. There's no other plausible explanation. But don't take my word for it. Check it out with Pierre at DDT."

"You're being facetious, Oliver. It's nothing to joke about. Pierre says it's a scientific fact that purple has the ability to turn dreamers into thinkers. Enough chatter for now. It's time for you to fill those bookshelves."

As always, he did exactly as Lula Weinberger demanded. With a knot in his gut, he dutifully unloaded his law books and filled the built-in library shelves.

****

Ten-year-old Alexandra ran into the house, bubbling with excitement and holding up a Mason jar full of tadpoles. She spotted her grandfather's plate turned upside down on the table and grinned. "Won't he be surprised?"

Dabney said, "Not only will he be surprised, he'll be very

proud of his little girl. Now, go wash up and get ready for supper."

Her forehead creased into a frown. "Am I really his little girl? Am I, Dabs?"

"Well, of course not. You're his big girl and growing like a weed. I had to sew a ruffle on the tail of your pink Sunday dress today. You've grown a couple of inches since I made it."

"That's not what I meant. Josie said her mother told someone on the telephone that she believes you're my real mother and that Daddy Mack's my real daddy and not my granddaddy and that's why you live with us."

Dabney's neck stiffened. People could say what they willed about her. She learned early in life to become accustomed to ridicule, but the thought of a few gossipy women spreading nasty rumors about Mack made her furious. "Seems Josie's mother is full of outlandish notions. Now, go do what I said before supper gets cold."

"Okay, but you know what? I wouldn't care if it was true. I wish you was my mama."

"But I'm not, and you know it. You had a beautiful mother named Zann and you are her spitting image."

"I wish I could remember her, but she died when I was born, right?"

Dabney nodded. "She lived just long enough to see how beautiful you were and to name you, honey. But she died shortly afterward."

"Daddy Mack said my daddy passed on before I was born.

18

Why is it when somebody dies, folks say they passed on?"

There was nothing Mack hated worse than a lie, but Dabney supposed he told the truth by telling Alexandra her daddy had passed on. Exactly where he'd passed on to was anyone's guess. The sorry rascal didn't waste any time hopping a train and getting out of town after he raped Zann. Her throat tightened. She turned her back and reached for the tea pitcher.

****

Oliver had been home six miserable weeks. He sat in his elaborate law office in the Weinberger Mansion in Goat Hill, Alabama, flipping through pages and pages of boring briefs. Was this all he had to look forward to? Day after day. Hour after hour. The only thing that ever changed in his life were the people who dribbled in, sometimes four in a week, sometimes less, but all with cases he was expected to miraculously fix in a courtroom. He threw the papers high in the air and watched them scatter over the floor.

The clients who came to him were anything but destitute. They were the rich getting richer by making the poor, poorer. The Depression had hit hard. People's farms were being repossessed without pity by the big wigs holding the notes—Oliver's clients.

His mother came clomping down the hall, and thrust open the door to his office. "Oliver, look at this mess on the floor. How many times must I tell you to keep the window near your desk closed? Besides, you know how susceptible you are to colds." She raised a brow, then slapped her hands together a couple of times— her way of demanding immediate action. "Well, why are you still sitting there as if you haven't heard a word I've said? This clutter has to be cleaned up."

With his elbows planted firmly on the desk, and his chin resting on clasped hands, Oliver didn't bother to look up. "Mother, get out."

Lula's shocked expression almost made him tack on an apology, but for once he let it stand.

Her distorted face slowly relaxed and she began picking up the strewn papers. "Well, I declare, aren't you the ornery one. I hope you aren't getting sick, dear. You look a little flushed. Perhaps you have a temperature." He jerked away when she placed the back of her hand against his forehead.

"I'm fine, mother. But I have things to do. Did you have a reason for coming into the office?"

"Yes, I almost forgot. Sallie Belle is coming home from Europe tomorrow, and I promised her mother you'd pick her up at the dock and bring her home to have dinner with us. Her boat will be arriving at 3:45."

"Sorry, no can do."

"What do you mean? Of course you can."

"Mother, I'll be in court tomorrow. I can't possibly be there to pick her up."

"Fiddlesticks. That can be taken care of and you know it. Simply call Judge Martin and tell him you need a postponement."

Oliver rolled his eyes. "I'm sorry, Mother. I know how important it is to you and Sallie for me to marry her, but it isn't gonna happen, so please stop pushing. Now, I'd appreciate it if you'd close the door on your way out." Noting her glare, he quickly added, "It's drafty in here. You know how susceptible I am to colds." He hated himself the moment the words left his lips. Why was he such a wimp?

****

Dabney dried her hands on the tail of her apron. "Alexandra, are you gonna stand there rambling all day, or do you intend to wash up as I asked you to do?"

"Sorry. I forgot." She ran out and came back to the table, holding up clean hands.

"Did you call your grandfather?"

"I did, but I think he's asleep. He didn't answer me."

Dabney pulled off her apron and hung it on a nail beside the sink. She walked back to the bedroom and knocked on the door. "Mack? Mack, supper's ready."

No answer.

"Mack, are you awake?" She eased the door open, then gasped, seeing him stretched out on the floor. "Alexandra," she screamed. "Run across the street and get Doc Williams. Tell him your granddaddy . . . your granddaddy is very sick."

Alexandra ran in the bedroom. "Why is he on the floor?"

"Go!" Dabney yelled. "Get Doc Williams. Quick."

Within minutes, the doctor was there, but Dabney knew—she knew even before he pulled the sheet over Mack's pale face. Their gaze locked and he simply nodded.

The skin around Dabney's eyes tightened as she searched the room with her eyes. "Where's Alexandra? Oh m'goodness, I've got to find her."

The doctor placed his hand on her back. "Alexandra's fine. My wife had just pulled a pound cake out of the oven, and she suggested Alexandra stay and have cake with Priscilla."

"Thank you. That was very kind. She and Priscilla play well together. I'm glad she's occupied for now, but poor kid is crazy about her Daddy Mack. She'll be devastated when she learns he's gone."

"I'm sure you both will draw comfort from one another. I understand you've been with the family for a long time?"

"Ten plus years."

"That *is* a long time. I'm sorry for your loss. Shall I lay him out on the dining table for you?"

"On the dining table?" Her voice quivered. "Why would you do that?"

"It'll be much easier for you to bathe and dress him on a solid surface."

She swallowed hard. *Bathe and dress? Me?* "But how will you pick him up?"

"I've lifted much heavier. My hands will almost reach around his waist. He must've lost ten pounds in the past few weeks."

"What do I do after . . . after he's dressed?"

"Eugene from the mortuary is over in Flat Creek setting up

another viewing, but he'll be back after lunch and you need to have the body bathed and dressed when he gets here. He'll want to know if you want a pine box or a fancier casket. Since the Reverend got most of his pay in chickens, eggs, syrup and the like, I'm sure there's not much money set aside in the sugar jar for fancy funerals. It's nothing to be ashamed of. Not many folks in these parts can afford anything more than the wooden box. Just tell Eugene which room you want the body to go in. I'd suggest this bedroom." He pointed toward the windows. "Maybe over there against the wall. That way it allows for a private viewing when you and the child wish to be alone with him, then you can open the bedroom door after folks start pouring in for the wake."

The doctor picked up Mack's lifeless body as if he were lifting a sack of guano, then carried him into the dining room, laid him on the table and placed two shiny pennies on his eyes. Watching the doctor drive away, she tried to remember all the instructions she was supposed to tell Eugene, but all she could remember was the instructions to bathe and dress Mack.

Alexandra came running through the house and headed for her grandfather's bedroom. "Where is he? Where's my Daddy Mack, Dabney? I was playing outside with Priscilla and I heard two men say he . . . he died. It's not true, is it? Did the doctor take him to the hospital?"

Dabney threw her arms around Alexandra and hugged her tightly. She led her over to the high-back rocker, and holding the precious little girl in her lap, gently stroked her long curls, while singing "Jesus Loves Me, This I Know."

Alex looked up into her eyes. "It's true, isn't it? Daddy Mack is . . . "

Dabney fought back the tears. "Yes, honey. Your Daddy Mack has gone on to be with Jesus."

Horrendous feelings of guilt overwhelmed her as she rocked back and forth, holding the sobbing child in her lap. Her focus should've been on comforting Alexandra, yet the thought of Mack in the next room, and the intimate details she was expected to perform, stole her thoughts from time to time. She could only imagine the gossip that would surely invade the community.

Then within minutes, two elders were knocking on the door, offering their services. News travels fast in a small community. Alexandra stayed close by Dabney's side, holding tightly on to her skirt tail, as if she were afraid that if she turned loose, the only person in the world she had left, might also disappear.

Dabney set out Mack's pin-striped suit, a white shirt and black tie, then gratefully handed the men the dishpan of warm water and a washrag.

Relieved, she reached down and held out her arms once more, to comfort a very distraught little girl.

Chapter Three

Oliver lumbered down the long corridor of the courthouse in painful silence with young Seth Sawyer. The steel taps on the bottom of Seth's resoled shoes made a loud clapping noise as the two attorneys walked in unintentional cadence, side by side.

The century-old building reeked of a mixture of cedar and Pine Oil. The further they walked, the louder the taps seemed to make on the polished pine floors. Oliver felt a strong need to apologize for winning, yet sensing the young attorney's pain, words seemed inadequate. What could he say? "You gave me a run for my money? Better luck next time? You weren't sufficiently prepared? I won because I have more experience? I went to Harvard, you didn't?"

Oliver was aware Seth wasn't seeking excuses or pats on the back, yet the tension between them thickened as they strolled in silence toward the front door of the Court House. Nearing the exit, Oliver sucked in a deep breath, and blurted, "Seth, I'm sorry.

Honestly, I am."

"Hey, man, no need to apologize." His voice quaked. "You're a good lawyer. A great lawyer. You won, I lost. That's how it goes."

Oliver pressed his lips together in a tight line. Somehow, he didn't feel much like a winner. Thanks to him, Hamm Dobson had just gained another farm he didn't need and Nonie Anderson and her children would likely be moving into the small shotgun house with her indigent parents.

That's how it goes. Seth's words haunted him like an annoying ghost with nothing to do but hang on his back to aggrieve him. What chance did the small farmers have in court with the court-appointed attorney who barely made it out of law school? Seth was young and inexperienced. Oliver had no doubt that one day the kid would be able to provide a decent defense, but by then, all the land in Goat Hill would be owned and occupied by four families—his, Hamm Dobson, Sallie Belle Sellers' parents and Kiah and Lizzie Grave.

Mentally drained, he drove home at a quarter 'til five with the intent of going straight to his room and falling across his bed with a good book. Anything to get his mind off the day's troubling events. Somehow, he had to get the picture of Nonie's pained-stricken face out of his head. A widow with five children. Why did Hamm need such a small plot of farmland? Why couldn't he have given her time for the harvest to come in, before foreclosing? *I keep wanting to blame Hamm, but I'm the one who sent Nonie packing. It's my fault. I took advantage of Seth's inexperience.* His stomach felt as if he'd swallowed a sack full of sandspurs.

"Ya-hoo? Is that you, dear?" Lula Weinberger called out, the minute he cracked open the front door.

"Yes, mother. Don't wait dinner on me. I'm whipped. Couldn't eat a thing. I'm going upstairs, to take a shower and—"

Sallie Belle rushed down the mammoth hall with open arms. "Oliver!" She squealed. "Surprise! I hope you missed me as much as I missed you." She twirled around. "Well, how do I look?"

"Uh . . . not a day older."

"You're such a riot. I was referring to my new duds and hairdo. I got a perm. You like it?"

"Uh-huh. Nice."

She grabbed his hand and pulled him toward the dining room. "Your mother told me your cook left this week, so Mama sent our cook over to make us dinner. We're having fried roe with scrambled eggs. It's one of Cloudy's specialties. And wait until you see what she's stirred up for dessert. Bread pudding."

"I'm sure it's delicious, but honestly, I can't eat a bite. I hope you and Mother will excuse me. I'm not feeling well. I barely made it through court today."

Lula made a clucking noise with her tongue. "My poor boy is all tuckered out. What you need is some food in that skinny body." She walked over and with her hands planted on his shoulders, pulled him to her level and kissed him on his cheek. With the back

27

of her hand placed on his forehead, she shook her head. "Nope! No fever. I'm sure you'll feel better after having a good meal, dear. Now, come have a seat at the table. Everything is ready. Would you prefer tea or coffee?"

Oliver lumbered over to the table, pulled out a chair for his mother and one for Sallie Belle, then fell like a limp ragdoll into the high-back mahogany chair next to the ornate empty chair at the head of the table, which remained reserved for his deceased father.

When the cook brought out a large platter of roe and eggs, Sallie took it and raked a generous portion on to Oliver's plate. "Take a bite and tell me what you think?"

He stuck his fork in the food and held his breath as he pushed it toward his mouth. Why didn't his mother tell Sallie he hated eggs? Ugh. Especially when scrambled with roe.

"Delicious?" She asked. "Cloudy is a wonderful cook. We're so fortunate to have her."

He swallowed without chewing. "It's been a long time since I've had anything like it."

"Oliver, your mother tells me you spend way too much time in your office. Now, that I'm here, I plan to help change that."

Oliver had known since high school Sallie Belle had her sights set for him, but to marry her would be like living with his domineering mother. He loved his mother, because . . . well . . . because she was his mother. But his feelings for Sallie Belle were platonic and nothing more. No doubt her feelings for him had nothing to do with love, but she'd been prepped since Junior High

28

that a union between the two families would be a smart business venture. It was all about money and prestige. He'd had his fill of both. Maybe money wasn't the root of his problem, but it had been the fertilizer that caused him to propagate into something he wasn't proud of. If only Sallie would give it up and go after someone who could share her ambitious goals.

Oliver sipped sweet tea from the crystal goblet. Why did he keep fooling himself with the idea that he'd one day find a woman who'd make his heart flutter, and his palms sweat when she walked in a room, the way it happens in books to couples in love? Even if he should find such a woman, she'd never be the type who'd feel the same way toward him. He once fooled himself into thinking he was in love. Lizzie Lancaster. What a beauty. They were even engaged for a while. A very short while. But Oliver never kidded himself into believing it was a match made in heaven. Not only was Lizzie not in love with him, his fascination with her had more to do with the way she drove his mother crazy. Her bull-headedness to stand up to Lula was the magnetic pull that drew her to him, even more than her gorgeous looks. If only he could be so bold. But Lizzie was the only person he'd ever met who would stand up to Lula Weinberger. He would've married her if she would've consented, even though he knew she was only going with him to make Kiah Grave jealous.

His throat tightened. What a coward he was. Why did he need a woman to rescue him from his mother's iron claws? Why couldn't he just walk out the door and never come back? He knew the answer. Because she was his mother. As much as he hated the life she'd carved out for him, there was no one who would ever love him the way she loved him. She meant well. If only she'd love him from afar instead of smothering him with her overbearing affection.

"Oliver Weinberger!" Lula scolded. "Sallie is talking to you. Where's your mind?"

"Forgive me. I'm tired and it's difficult to concentrate." He glared at his Mother. "I know what you're thinking. Don't say it. It's all because I threw out the purple chair."

"Go ahead and mock Pierre, but I have definitely noticed a gradual lapse in judgement, since you brought in that common, leather chair. You can't deny that you've become much more absent-minded lately." Lula placed her hand on top of Sallie Belle's. "Excuse us for interrupting, dear. Now, what were you saying to Oliver?"

"I said all work and no play makes Oliver a dull boy. So beginning tomorrow, I plan to see that he start having a little fun. I'll have Cloudy prepare us a picnic lunch and we'll go down to the river and have a picnic. Doesn't that sound lovely, Oliver?"

"I'm sorry, Sallie, my schedule is full. Why don't you call Rollo? He's asked about you several times since you've been away. I'm sure he'd love to accompany you on a picnic."

She sat there looking stunned. "You're kidding, right? Me and Rollo Treadwell? Not on your life. If you can't go tomorrow, we'll go the next day."

"No, Sallie. Not tomorrow not the next day and not next week." He slammed his napkin on the table. "Now, if you ladies will excuse me, I need to retire to my room. It's been a very trying day."

Sallie's mouth gaped open. "Well, I never."

Lula rose from the table. "Excuse me, Sallie. I'm afraid my boy is even more fatigued than I realized. He's not acting like himself."

Oliver was half-way up the stairs when he heard Sallie whine, "I've never been so humiliated in my life. Purple chair or no purple chair, exhaustion is no excuse for bad manners."

Chapter Four

Within the hour, the Parsonage was filled with grieving people coming to stay the night for the traditional wake. They brought bowls and platters laden with all sorts of delicious food and shared heart-wrenching, emotional stories about how Parson Pruitt's influence had enriched their lives.

Dabney walked around in a fog. She was touched that the parishioners had taken over the unpleasant task of planning the funeral, freeing her to spend time with Alexandra, who clung to her like beggar lice on cotton socks. How could she explain to a child why God chose to take her grandfather, when she couldn't understand it herself? Mack would've known what to say. He always seemed to have the answers. But Dabney had pressing questions of her own. What would happen to a child with no parents and whose only known relative was locked away in an asylum? Her answer came too quickly. The orphanage. Of course. The taste of hot bile rose to her throat. *No. They can't. She'll stay with me. They can't take her away. I won't let them!*

It wasn't until after the service, as Dabney walked across the road from the church cemetery that one of the elders stopped her. Stunned, it took a few moments for his words to sink in.

"Miss Foxworthy, it pains me to bring this up at a time such as this, but I think it only fair to give you as much time as possible to plan your next move. As you know, the parsonage belongs to the church, and now with the Parson Pruitt gone, we'll be looking for a new pastor, who of course will move into the house."

She stared at him without blinking. With all that had happened, she hadn't taken time to consider that she'd have to find a place to live. "Of course." The muscles in her face twitched.

"Ma'am, I know this has been sudden and you've had no time to prepare, so we'd like to extend you thirty days occupancy to make plans for your future. I am so sorry. I understand you've been with the family for a very long time, and I know this must be an awful shock. If we can assist you in moving, we have men willing to help."

Help move? Where would she go? How would she support Alexandra? The last question, the one that troubled her most, would have to be answered to the satisfaction of Agnes McAdams from the Child Welfare Department.

That night at supper, Alexandra picked at her food. She'd barely eaten anything since finding her father on the floor. "Dabs, can I sleep in Daddy Mack's bed tonight?"

"Of course, you can, sweetheart. Would you like me to sleep

with you?"

She shook her head. "No thanks. I just want to be by myself."

Dabney feigned a smile. "I understand. But if you decide to come sleep with me, it'll be fine."

At two a.m. Dabney opened her eyes to find Alexandra standing over her, pulling on the sleeve of her flannel nightgown. "Wake up, Dabs. I have something to show you. Something real important. Turn on the light so you can see."

"Sweetheart, can't it wait until morning?"

"No, I want to show you what I found. You gotta see this."

The sheer excitement in her voice made it impossible for Dabney to ignore her. "I thought you were going to sleep. What have you been doing in there?"

Plopping down on the bed, Alexandra held an envelope to her chest, and gushed. "There was a hat box on Daddy Mack's bed, and . . . and it had pictures in it . . . and . . . and I couldn't go to sleep so I poured everything out on the bed and guess what?"

"I don't know, sweetie, but we've had a long day, so why don't we talk about it tomorrow?" She covered her mouth with her hand and yawned. I'm really tired and you need to go to sleep, also."

The words seemed lost on the enthusiastic little girl. Once again, she jerked at Dabney's sleeve. "Dabs, open your eyes. Please? This is important."

With eyelids at half-mast, Dabney muttered, "Fire away, I'm

listening, but make it snappy. I was awake all last night, honey, and I can't hold my eyes open much longer."

"Okay, I'll talk fast." She reached over and switched on the lamp.

Dabney squinted at the bright light and covered her eyes with her hand.

"So I found a hatbox with pictures and stuff in it, and—"

"You said that already, Alexandra." Dabney groaned at the sharpness in her voice. The child had just suffered a great loss. Her exuberance struck Dabney as a bit peculiar, but perhaps Alex was handling her grief in the only way she knew how—replacing thoughts that were too painful to deal with, with happy thoughts. "Tell me quickly, then let's get some shut-eye."

"Thanks, Dabs. So I pulled out the pictures . . . oops! Did I say that already?"

"Doesn't matter, sweetheart. Go ahead and tell me. I'm listening."

"Well, some of the snapshots were of me and some of Daddy Mack, and I think a few were of Mama Pruitt, but I'm not sure, because I don't really remember what she looked like. Did she have red hair?"

Dabney's eyes narrowed. "I'm sorry. I didn't mean to close my eyes. What did you say?"

"Mama Pruitt. Was her hair red?"

"Yes. A very pretty shade of red. I'm glad you enjoyed looking at all the family pictures. Now, why don't you crawl in the bed with me and let's get some sleep and I promise you, tomorrow we'll look at the pictures together." She pulled the covers back, urging Alex to crawl under.

"Wait. You didn't see what I found. It has my mama on it."

"But your Daddy Mack has shown you pictures of your mother before and I remember what she looked like. She was very pretty. Just like you."

"You don't have to pretend any longer, Dabs. I know the truth. The whole truth." She grabbed Dabney around the neck and clung to her. "I love you, Mama."

"Your mama loved you, too, darling." Dabney held her close for a few minutes, stroking her long blonde locks. "Can you reach the lamp?"

Alex switched out the light and snuggled up beside Dabney. "Dabs, why did you and Daddy Mack keep it from me? Why didn't you want me to know who my real mother was? Did you think I was too young to understand? I'm smart for my age, you know."

"I know you are, sweetheart, but we told you the truth." Dabney was no longer sleepy. She sat up and switched the lamp back on. "Honey, your Daddy Mack told you your mama died. That *is* the truth. The real truth. Now, why would you think he didn't tell you everything? Let me see the picture."

"What picture."

"The one of your mother."

"Oh, I'll have to go get them. I left them on Daddy Mack's

36

bed."

Dabney glanced down at a manila envelope in Alex's hand. "But I thought . . ." Then, gazing into those big blue eyes, she tried to remember the confusing conversation. What had she missed? "Don't you have a picture of your mother in the envelope? I thought you said you wanted me to see her picture."

"No. I said I was looking through pictures, when I found it."

"Found it? Found what, sweetheart?"

"This." She thrust the envelope toward Dabney.

Dabney reached in and pulled out a yellowed document. The letterhead bore the name of a hospital in New Orleans, Louisiana. *A birth certificate?* She tried to hide her shock. Why now, with so many other things to deal with, did this have to appear? She read the name on the first line. Mother: DABNEY FOXWORTHY.

Dabney could understand why Zann used her name at the Home for Unwed Mothers. After all, the whole idea was to convince people in Pivan Falls that she—not Zann—was the one pregnant, and to leave the impression the Reverend Pruitt and his wife were adopting her baby.

But the greatest shock was in bold letters on the second line. Father: KIAH GRAVE. *Kiah?* No. No, no, no! It wasn't possible. Why would Zann put Kiah's name on the birth certificate? Her eyes quickly skimmed the page. Baby girl, 5 lbs. 2 oz, Name: ALEXANDRA GRAVE. And what reason would she have for giving Alexandra his last name, unless— No, it couldn't be true. Zann wouldn't have lied about being raped by Arnold Evers. Not even to save Kiah's skin. *Would she?*

.

Two wide, blue orbs glared down at her, appearing to wait for an explanation. "Dabs, you look sad. Are you mad I found out?"

Dabney wrapped her arms around her. "Oh, no, sweetheart. You deserve to know the truth." As soon as the words escaped her lips, Dabney winced. How could she tell the child the truth if she wasn't convinced she knew it herself? "But it's late, Alex, so go back to bed and let's get some sleep. You have school tomorrow, and when you come home, we'll both be rested and can talk about this."

Relieved when it seemed to satisfy, Dabney now had ten or twelve hours to mull it over before blurting something she might later regret.

Chapter Five

Dabney had just waved Alexandra off to school, when Ed Blocker, one of the elders from the church showed up at the door. Her temples throbbed.

Whatever he'd come for would not be good news. That, she knew for sure. She only hoped he wouldn't hem- haw around the subject, but would come right out and state his business to keep her from fretting any longer.

"Good morning, Miss Foxworthy. It's such a beautiful day, do you mind if we sit on the porch while I state my business for being here?"

She cleared her throat and attempted to mask her fear. "Good morning, Mr. Blocker. Have a seat in the glider and I'll go inside a get you a cup of coffee."

"Only if it's made. Wouldn't want to put you out."

"The pot's still on the stove. I'll pour us both a cup."

Unable to stop her hands from shaking, the cup made a rattling sound on the saucer as she handed it to her guest. Had he come to tell her the elders changed their minds about allowing her thirty days to find a place to live? "What's on your mind, Mr. Blocker?" She braced, waiting for an answer she was confident she didn't want to hear.

"First, Miss Foxworthy, I must tell you that no one is more distressed over this situation than I. We can't always understand why bad things happen to good people. And I don't reckon I've ever met a finer man than the Reverend Pruitt."

Dabney pressed her lips together. Why was he hedging? "Mr. Blocker, whatever you've come to say, please don't hesitate. I know you're only doing your job by coming here."

He stuck his hand in his breast pocket. "Thank you, you're right in thinking I was sent here to perform a task. The church called a special business meeting last night, and we've taken up a small offering to help tide you over until you can find employment." He handed her an envelope.

She tried to convince herself she had to be strong. Couldn't cry. Not here. Not now. But in spite of her best efforts, giant tears seeped from her eyes. Before she could properly thank him, he said, "And there's one more thing." Dabney held her breath, waiting for instructions to vacate immediately.

"I don't know if you're aware, but Chuck Hogan held the note on Pastor Pruitt's car. Now that the preacher's gone, the car goes back to Chuck, but he's made out a Bill of Sale to you, *Paid in Full.*"

She fought the urge to throw her arms around the man for bringing such great news and afterward she'd like to go find the generous fellow who would do something so wonderful for someone he hardly knew. She'd seen Mr. Hogan at church, but except for a casual greeting, they'd never even spoken. Would these wonderful people have been so generous, if they knew the tainted reputation she left behind in Pivan Falls? Since moving to Foggy Bottom seven years ago, it felt as if she'd been given a second chance. Sure, there were a couple of nosey biddies who scoffed at the idea of a young woman living in the same house with their pastor, while his wife was away at a hospital, but the church's generosity proved that not everyone bought in to the ill-founded rumors. The day Mack accepted the call, he told them his daughter died giving birth, the father was no longer in the picture and he and Dora were raising the child. Not a lie, and no one seemed to question the circumstances.

"Mr. Blocker, I don't know what to say."

He winked. "Just say, thank-you, Lord, and that'll be sufficient."

After he left, Dabney stuck the Bill of Sale in her pocket and tore open the envelope to find two-hundred dollars and thirty-five cents inside. "Thank you, Lord, thank you, Lord, thank you, Lord."

Her newfound joy was quick-lived when she looked out the window and saw a dark blue Studebaker pull up in the front yard. She squinted trying to recognize the stout, white-haired lady getting out of the automobile. *Oh, no! Not her*. Her pulse raced as she watched Agnes McAdams from the Child Welfare Department lug a large leather brief case out of the car—a not-so-gentle reminder that this was not going to be a neighborly visit. Dabney's first instinct was to avoid answering the door, yet in her heart she knew it would only be prolonging the inevitable. Sooner or later, she'd have to face the woman.

"Dabney, may I come in?"

As much as she liked Agnes as a friend, she wanted to stomp her foot and shriek, "No. Go away. Leave us alone." Instead, she drew a deep breath and nodded. "Come on in, Agnes and have a seat."

"I suppose you know this is not a personal call."

"I know. I've been expecting you."

"It's my job, Dabney."

"Agnes, I know you're here on Alexandra's behalf, but you have nothing to worry about. Her grandmother's in the hospital, you know, and until she comes home, I'll continue serving as Alexandra's nursemaid. Wherever I go, I'll take her with me and care for her the same way I've done all her life."

"I wish it were that simple, Dabney." She unbuckled the briefcase and pulled out a binder. "Our office has contacted the asylum, and according to the doctor there, Mrs. Pruitt is terminally insane and will never leave Bryce's, but I'm sure you know that already." She thumbed through a few pages. "I have the report if you wish to read it."

"That won't be necessary. I trust you, Agnes."

"Thank you. I'll have to say, I've dealt with some difficult cases during my tenure, but I can't tell you how hard this was for me to come here today. I know how much you love the child. But with Alexandra's grandfather gone, it's up to us to place her."

Agnes dug around in her pocketbook, pulled out a linen handkerchief and handed it to Dabney.

"Agnes, please. I know you're only doing your job, but you've got to help me. Please, please don't let them put her in an orphanage. I'll do anything I have to do to be able to keep her with me."

She reached for Dabney's hand and gave a gentle squeeze. "Oh, honey, you know if there was anything I could do, I would. But my hands are tied. The decision isn't mine to make."

"I'm sorry, but there has to be something that can be done. Agnes, I can't let her be shipped off to an orphanage."

"Well, let's see what we might can do to avoid that. Do you happen to know if the child has any relatives? Grandparents? Aunts, uncles? Someone who might be willing to take her?"

Dabney shook her head. "Pastor Pruitt's folks died of the flu in 1917. Mrs. Pruitt was an only child and her parents are both dead. I'm not aware of any relatives and I've been with them for ten years. But why would the department be agreeable to send her to live with relatives she's never known, rather than allow her to live with me, when I'm the one who has taken care of her since the day she was born? It doesn't make sense. I'm perfectly capable of taking care of Alexandra."

43

"I know you'd try."

"Agnes, please, I'm begging you. I'll find a good-paying job. There are plenty of people here in Foggy Bottom who'll gladly give me references."

"But who'd be taking care of Alexandra while you're working? These are the type questions the agency has to have answers to, and as much as I wish it weren't so, I don't think you can answer them."

"I'll get a job working for a wealthy family who'll allow Alexandra and me to live in a guest house. We'll manage. You'll see."

"Oh, honey, I wish I could, but you don't understand my position. I can't even get you approved as a temporary foster home. Through no fault of your own, you've been left with no place to live and no job. Now, if you were married—with a breadwinner in the family—you'd stand a much better chance. But as it stands, the department has rules that we must abide by. I'm so sorry. What time does she usually get home from school? I'll come back, but you'll need to have her bags packed."

Dabney's breath came out in short, fast pants. "You can't, Agnes. You can't take her away from me. Can't you make them understand? I've mothered her for ten years."

Agnes shoved the binder back into the briefcase and stood to leave. "I'm so sorry, Dabney. You know I'd help you if I could. I'll be back for her around four o'clock."

Desperation jerked at Dabney's heartstrings. "Do you really

44

mean that? You'd help if you could? Hold on. I have something to show you." She ran in the bedroom and grabbed the birth certificate. Shoving it into Agnes's hands, she held her breath as Agnes studied it for what seemed a good five minutes before she opened her mouth.

"Oh, Dabney." She thrust her hand over her heart. "You're her mother! No wonder your heart is breaking. That changes things, for sure."

Dabney could hear Mack's voice as clearly as if he were in the room. *No more lies.* "Agnes, I didn't say I was the mother."

Her brow furrowed as her gaze focused on the paper in her hand. "I'm confused. This is a legal birth certificate. Perhaps you had your own reasons for not wanting anyone to know before now, but with this proof, there's no court in the land that would take Alexandra away from you."

Was a deception the same as a lie? Would Mack approve? Aren't some lies worse than others? No question about it, Mack wouldn't want someone putting his little girl in a home with strangers. Yet, the unwelcome, grating voice kept playing in her head. *No more lies.*

Agnes smiled. "This is all I need to close the case. I'll simply write, 'The child is with her birth mother. But why did you hesitate to give it to me? I gather she was born out of wedlock?"

Dabney blurted, "I hesitated, because what's on that paper is a lie." The abrupt admission caused her heart to palpitate. She'd hoped she'd feel all clean inside, once she told the truth, but in

45

fact, she felt worse. Much worse.

"You're shaking, Dabney." Agnes took her by the arm and led her to a chair. "Now, would you like to explain?"

"No. And that's the truth. I wouldn't like to explain, because to do so would be breaking a confidence."

Agnes knelt in front of her and holding Dabney's shaking hands in hers, she whispered. "No explanation necessary. But if you don't mind, I'll borrow this copy. I'll mimeograph it and mail it back to you. If I don't see you and Alexandra again, I'll be praying for you both. I'd love to hear from you after you get settled somewhere."

"If you don't see us? After we settle? What are you saying?"

"I'm saying you won't be hearing from my office again. Take care of that sweet little girl. Don't bother to get up to see me out. You look pale. I think you'd better sit there for a while."

After Agnes left, Dabney sat for an hour, going over the conversation. Mack was right. The truth is always better than a lie. He would've been proud of her. However, she had another hurdle to face at three-fifteen. How could she explain the truth to Alexandra, without giving too much information to an innocent ten-year-old?

Chapter Six

Oliver arose early Thursday morning and dressed in the tailored suit his mother had hung on the oak valet the night before. He put on the argyle socks she purchased from Sears and Roebuck and laced up the black wingtips she ordered from Macys.

Standing in front of the bathroom mirror, he poured a little Vitalis in his hands and rubbed through his hair. Then parting it in the middle he combed it in the same slicked-down style his father had always worn his hair. He picked up the wire-rimmed spectacles, which he didn't need, but according to his mother, made him look respectable.

"Fauntleroy," he sneered at the milksop image staring back at him in the mirror. He trudged down the long stairs and made his way into the kitchen to sit in the same chair in the same house facing the same window, where he'd sat for his entire twenty-seven years. His father's place at the table had been at the end, with his beside him. Now, his father's heavy, carved oak chair sat empty. His mother treated it as a shrine, often talking to the empty chair.

After breakfast, Oliver would walk to the garage, get in his car, drive to the Court House and face Seth to argue the case on the day's docket. He'd win, of course. And he'd die a little more inside, feeling like a chump. He'd return home, sit down at the same long banquet table to share dinner with his mother, who sat so far on the opposite end that he could barely carry on a conversation without shouting. She'd ask about his day, and praise him for winning. She'd suggest a game of Gin Rummy and he'd let her win. He'd retire to his room with a book and read until he fell asleep. This was his life—his past, his present and his future.

"Oliver?" His mother stood at the bottom of the stairs. "What kept you? There's no excuse for tardiness. You know breakfast is served at six-thirty sharp. I expect you to be prompt. A man who dawdles is a man who loses the respect of his peers."

"Respect of my peers?" Oliver let out a chuckle that turned into raucous laughter. He couldn't seem to stop.

"I declare, I don't know what gets into you, sometimes, dear. What did I say that you find so humorous?"

"You're worried that I'll lose the respect of my peers? Really? And who do you consider my peers?"

"Why . . . Judge Martin for one."

"For one? Is that all you can come up with? Mother, Judge Martin is forty years older than me. The only thing we have in common is that we both have a law degree and a pedigree. Can you

48

come up with another, please? I'd really like to know which of my peers you feel I need to impress."

"You're talking crazy, Oliver. Now, cease the nonsense and eat your breakfast. That is, if you can stomach these lumpy grits. I declare, this new cook manages to ruin everything she tries to prepare. Never seen a woman who couldn't boil water without scorching it. But we won't have to put up with her any longer."

Oliver bit his tongue. He had already said more than he'd intended.

"Besides not being able to cook, she's such a ninny. She jerked off her apron, threw it on the floor and slammed the back door on her way out, after I tactfully complained about the grits. But the ad is still running in the newspaper. People harp on hard times, but if jobs are so hard to come by, why can't I find a cook willing to work? Too many lazy folks in this world, that's why."

Oliver had his own theory of why his mother had trouble keeping a cook and it had nothing to do with laziness. Goat Hill wasn't so big that testimonies from past servants didn't circulate faster than a wildfire.

Chapter Seven

Dabney sat rocking on the porch, counting every dreaded minute as she waited for Alexandra to get home from school. She'd spent the morning rehearsing the anticipated conversation, which would soon take place—carefully and painstakingly going over answers to awkward questions that were sure to come.

How much information was too much? Could she satisfy the child's curiosity without revealing the gruesome details concerning her birth? Her heart beat erratically when she spotted Alexandra running down the road. "Wisdom, Lord," she prayed. "Give me wisdom."

Alexandra pounced up the steps with her arms open wide. "Hi, Dabs. Remember your promise?"

"Of course, I remember. But first, wouldn't you like to go inside, have a snack and tell me about your day?"

"No ma'am. I'm not hungry. Let's sit here. I want you to tell me all about my daddy. It's all I've thought about all day." She dropped her books on the porch and plopped down in the swing. "Was he handsome? Do I look like him, 'cause I don't look like you one bit. I wouldn't care if I did, though, 'cause you're real pretty."

Dabney quickly lifted up a silent prayer. *Help me, Lord.* "Alexandra, I wish we could've waited a few more years to have this conversation, but since it's come up, I think your grandfather would want me to tell you the truth, or at least as much as you can understand for the time being."

"I'm not a little kid, Dabs, you can tell me anything. I know you weren't married because you and my daddy don't have the same last name. That's why you kept it a secret, isn't it? Well, I don't care. I'm glad you're my mama. Did you love my daddy?"

Dabney was thankful Alexandra was too enamored with the idea of having a father to wait for an answer to the last question, which Dabney wasn't ready to give.

"I think he had a very romantic name, don't you? Kiah Grave." She folded her hands under her chin and swooned. "Sounds like a movie star. You know, like Clark Gable. I'll bet he was handsome." She tilted her head and the name rolled off her tongue in whispered repetition. "Kiah Grave. Kiah Grave. I love saying his name. Isn't it beautiful? When did he die, Dabney?"

Mack's words rang in her ears as plainly as if he were standing next to her. *No more lies.* "Sweetheart, Kiah isn't dead." Her pulse raced. *Mack, this is so unfair. Why did you leave me with this overwhelming responsibility?*

"Well, blow me down. Are you serious?" Alex squealed with delight. "That's terrific. I can't believe it. When Granddaddy said he passed on, I thought he meant my daddy died. Where did he pass on to? Can I meet him?"

Dabney's eyes rolled back in her head. Apparently the child chose to ignore the truth and believe what she wanted to believe. Her words spilled out so fast, Dabney could hardly keep up.

"Oh, and Dabs, I've been thinking—now that I know the truth, shouldn't I call you Mama?"

Filling her lungs with air, Dabney slowly exhaled. She wrapped an arm around the wide-eyed little girl and gave her a squeeze. "No, sweetheart. You shouldn't, because you had a mama and I'm not her. Your grandfather told you the truth when he told you your mother was his beautiful daughter, Zann, and you're her spittin' image."

Alex sailed out of the swing, and with her hands planted on her hips, squawked, "That's a big fat lie. I saw my birth certificate. Why don't you just tell the truth? You didn't want me when I was born, so you gave me to Granddaddy and Grandmother. Well, I'll run away and sneak Grandmother out of the hospital. I'm gonna go live with her. You don't love me."

"Alexandra, sit back down. You said you weren't a little kid, but you're acting like one. If you want to have this conversation, you need to show me you're mature enough to understand. Now, shall we continue?"

Crossing her arms over her chest, she nodded and sat down,

snubbing. "*Do* you love me?"

"Honey, I love you across the ocean and back, but love has nothing to do with the truth." Dabney sucked in a lungful of air and silently sent up a prayer. "Your mother was my best friend. I would've done anything for her. And I did."

"What do you mean?"

Dabney's pulse raced. She reached and grasped Alex's hand and mused at how small it was. Was she crazy for attempting this conversation? She had only one chance to get this right. What if she botched it?

"Sweetheart, your mother was my best friend and the sweetest person I've ever known. But one day, she found out she was gonna have a baby."

Alex's face twisted. "Me?"

"Yes, I'm taking about you. But—" Dabney closed her eyes, afraid to go on and afraid to stop. "You see, sweetie, your mother wasn't married, and, well, you know God's plan is for a woman to get married first and then have a baby. Not the other way around." Her throat couldn't have ached more if she'd swallowed razor blades. Where could she go from here? Had she said too much already? Would Mack have approved? "I don't know how to say this, so be patient and try to understand, okay?"

"Don't worry, I know all about where babies come from. Josie told me."

Dabney's eyes popped open. She wished she could've explained the birds and bees before that twelve-year-old know-it-all, Josie Roundtree, gave Alex her perverted version. "As I was saying, when the sequence doesn't follow God's plan, sometimes people can be cruel and place blame, where blame is not due."

"So people were mad at my mama because she was PG?"

Dabney flinched, hearing Alex use the slang term for pregnant. But now was not the time to reprimand. Exactly how much had Josie told her?

"No one was angry at your mama, because no one even knew she was gonna have a baby. No one but me and your grandparents. Zann left Pivan Falls that summer, before she began to show."

Her eyes widened. "You said you did something for her. I think I get it. You told people I was your baby, so they wouldn't be mad with mama. That's right, isn't it?"

The kid took after Zann. She was smart. Much smarter than Dabney had given her credit for.

"Yes, honey, that's exactly what I did. I wore maternity clothes while she was gone, so folks would think I was the one pregnant."

"But why would you lie about something like that? Didn't they say bad things about *you* when they thought you were PG and not married?"

"Alex, I wish you wouldn't use that term."

"Josie says it all the time."

"Well, you don't need to do everything Josie does."

"Okay. But I sure wouldn't lie for somebody if it made people think I was the one who was bad."

54

"Alexandra, lying is always wrong. Your grandfather didn't like the idea, but I went against him because I wanted to save your mother's reputation. You see, honey, she was a good girl. Never did anything bad. But I was different back then, so people already looked down on me. If they thought I was pregnant, no one would bat an eye, because they expected no better of me. Zann's good-girl reputation would remain intact. I did it because I loved your mother. She treated me like I was somebody."

"But you are somebody."

Was she getting through or talking in circles? "I think I've answered all your questions, so why don't we go in the house and have some cookies and milk?"

Alexandra followed her into the kitchen.

Dabney sat out the cookies and milk, and then scooped out enough flour from the flour bin into a bowl to make biscuits for supper.

Dunking a cookie in milk, Alex said, "Dabs, I want to know all about my mother. Daddy Mack showed me her pictures, but I want you to tell me what she was like, since you were her best friend."

Dabney let out a breath. Getting the kid to understand why Zann's name wasn't on the birth certificate had been much easier than she'd imagined. All her fretting had been in vain. "I'd love to tell you about your mama. She was beautiful, and you look just like her. She was also very smart, and oh my goodness, everyone loved Zann Pruitt."

Alex's face lit up. "Did she have a boyfriend?"

"You are such a little romantic. Yes, she was in love with a very nice boy who was in her class at school." Without looking up, Dabney kept rolling out biscuits, before she stopped to think that she didn't need a baker full, now that Mack was gone.

"Was his name Kiah Grave?"

"As a matter of fact, it was Kiah."

"I thought so. He was my daddy, you know."

The birth certificate! "Well, I don't think we should jump to conclusions. After all, my name was on it, also, and I'm not your mother."

"But it's true. He's my daddy and I know it, because girls get PG when—sorry, Dabs. I mean they get that way when they're in love and, you know . . . kiss. Besides, why would she put another man's name on the birth certificate if he wasn't my daddy? I imagine he was really, really sad when she died and he couldn't keep me. I'll bet he wanted to, but it'd be hard for a man to keep a newborn baby and go to work, you know."

Dabney mulled over the conversation. Had she lied? No. Alex had made her own assumptions. Why not let it go at that? What harm could there be in the child believing she had a loving father who would've kept her if he could have? She recalled the pain of her own childhood, when the one thing she wanted more than anything in the whole world was a daddy. A real daddy. Though her mother had been dead over fourteen years, the stinging bitterness remained as Dabney relived those younger years when

56

men blew into their little shanty at Rooster Run, like houseflies—in through the front door and out through the back, all coming for a little "sugar." There was one in particular she even called Daddy, only to learn he was no different from the rest. It hurt. Hurt bad.

Dabney lay awake most of the night, reading and re-reading the yellowed letter that Zann gave her shortly before she drew her last breath, over ten years ago.

My dearest Dabney,

My heart is heavy as I write this letter, but it's also filled with love and gratitude for what you were willing to do for me. I was wrong in allowing it, and I am so sorry. I thought I was doing it for Daddy, knowing it could hurt his ministry if people discovered I was pregnant, but deep down, I know I was doing it for my own prideful reasons. I was embarrassed over the situation I found myself in and feared the stigma of being raped and the gossip which would surely follow. But to let you put yourself up for ridicule for my sake was selfish of me. You're the best friend I've ever had.

The doctors won't tell me, but I know I'm dying. Mother and Daddy will be the guardians of my precious baby, but should anything ever happen to them, please promise me you'll keep up with Kiah's whereabouts, and take the child to him. I know if the time should ever come, he'll take good care of our baby.

All my love,

Zann

She had no idea where Kiah might be. The last she knew, he'd gone to Goat Hill, Alabama, to meet his father. Her throat ached anew when she recalled the day he left—the shameless way she clung to him, begging to go with him, though she knew he didn't love her. *Oh, how I loved that man.* She couldn't deny any excuse to see him once more caused the hairs on the back of her neck to prickle.

Never could she have imagined a day would come when she'd be obligated to keep the promise, since she expected Mack to live forever. *Zann trusted me.* That settled it. Somehow, she'd find him. They'd have a nice little reunion, she'd show him the letter, and being single, he'd feel terrible for not being in a position to honor such an unreasonable request. She'd assure him she understood. After all, Zann was very young and under duress when she wrote the letter. Still, there was one tiny, three-letter word at the bottom of the page that troubled her. Strange, she hadn't noticed when she first read it. Why did Zann say, "I know he'll take good care of *our* baby?"

Dabney didn't like the crazy questions surfacing. *I'm putting too much emphasis on one little word. Zann was raped. And not by Kiah.* Why couldn't she let it go at that?

Dabney awoke early the next morning, choosing to stay in bed and bask in the memory of the most incredible dream. *I found Kiah and when he learned Alexandra thought he was her father, he said it would be cruel to tell her differently . . . it wasn't as if we'd lied to her. He said he realized after he left Pivan Falls that he loved me and should've taken me with him to Goat Hill. Then I dreamed he said . . .* She blotted the tears with the corner of the bedsheet. *He said we should get married and give Alexandra the loving home that Zann would've wanted for her.* Her heart beat faster. "What if . . . ?"

She jumped up, reached in the top of the closet and pulled down a suitcase.

Alexandra woke up at 8:15 and ran through the house, yelling. "Dabs, look at the clock, I'm late for school."

"You won't be going to school, today, sweetheart."

"But it's not a holiday. And why are you packing our clothes?"

"We're taking a trip."

"A trip? Swell! Where we going?"

"To a place called Goat Hill to visit an old friend."

Chapter Eight

"This is Goat Hill?" Alex craned her neck, looking out the open window.

Dabney forced a smile, though her insides trembled. "I believe it is."

"Where does your friend live?"

"Not sure." She pointed ahead. "There's a diner. Why don't we park, go in and get a bite. You hungry?"

"Starving."

The restaurant was small, but the white and aqua tiles gave it a clean, sparkly look. Dabney and Alexandra took a seat near the plate-glass window. A middle-aged waitress popping chewing gum as if it were an art and wearing far too much makeup walked over and plopped two menus on the table. "What can I get ya'?"

Alex said, "Dabs, maybe she knows where your friend lives. Why don't you ask her?"

Dabney ignored the question and glanced over the fare. "Two hamburgers, all the way, a grape soda and a cup of coffee, please."

The waitress said, "Kid's prob'ly right. I reckon I know most folks from these parts. Who ya' looking for?"

Dabney winced. "Thank you, but I'm sure I'll have no trouble." She hoped she hadn't sounded snooty, but she wasn't ready to trust Alex's reaction by mentioning Kiah's name in public. What was she thinking by coming here, anyway? She knew the answer. It was that silly dream. How long is one obligated to keep a promise to the dead? And why was she prolonging telling Alex that Kiah wasn't her father? She needed to explain before she let them meet. *Explain? How?*

By the time Dabney's food arrived, she was no longer hungry. How could she eat with so much on her mind? Was it the promise to Zann that brought her here . . . or a deep longing to see the only man she'd ever loved? It'd been ten years. What if he was married? She debunked the notion. *He was too in love with Zann to give his heart to another woman.* Dabney had always believed had he not met Zann first, he would've fallen in love with her. She swallowed the lump in her throat. *But he did meet Zann first. Who could compete with someone so perfect?*

Alex took a bite of her hamburger. "Dabs, why didn't you tell the waitress who you're looking for?"

"Don't talk with your mouth full." She jerked around, hearing a man's voice call out her name.

"Dabney Foxworthy? Land sakes alive, is it really you?" Looking as handsome as ever, Kiah Grave walked over with open arms. "You look fantastic. Stand up and give me a hug. What are you doing here?"

Alexandra piped up. "We're here to visit her friend, but we don't know where she lives."

He looked down. "And who are you, cutie?" The words barely escaped when his eyes squinted and his face paled. He glared at Dabney. "She's . . . ?"

Dabney nodded. Her legs were too weak to continue standing.

When Kiah rocked back on his feet, Dabney grabbed his arm. "You okay?"

He whispered, "I feel as if I've seen a ghost. She looks so much like . . . like her mother."

Alex wiped her mouth with a napkin and looked up. "What did you say about my mother?"

"I said you're beautiful like your mother. Same hair, same eyes, same gorgeous smile. It's like looking at Zann."

"Thank you. She died soon after I was born. Did you know that? How did you know her?"

Dabney grimaced and shook her head in slow motion. He must've seen the panic in her eyes.

"Uh . . . we went to school together."

Dabney attempted to turn the conversation, but Alex wasn't ready to drop it. In between bites of her hamburger, she blurted, "Did you know my daddy, mister? His name's Kiah Grave and my name's Alexandra Grave. What's yours?"

"Pruitt!" Dabney blurted. "Your name is Alexandra Pruitt, and you know it." Dabney found it impossible to discern whether the strange expression on Kiah's face was one of anger, shock or hope.

Alex shrugged. "Pruitt is my adopted name. My mama and daddy weren't married when I was born. That probably shocks you, doesn't it? But I don't care. My granddaddy once told me the Bible says nobody's perfect." She took a big swig of grape soda.

He nodded. "Your grandfather was a wise man, Alexandra, but I expect your mother came as close to being perfect as anyone I've ever known. I have some grown-up business to discuss with Dabney and there's a Three Stooges movie on at the picture show across the street. Here's a dime. Why don't you run watch it, and we won't bore you with our business."

"Gee, thanks, mister. Can I go to the movie, Dabs?"

"Sure. Be careful crossing the street and as soon as it's over, come straight back to the cafe."

Kiah leaned forward, then glanced around, making sure no one was in hearing distance. "You must know my head is swimming. What's this all about?"

"Kiah, you're the reason I'm here. We need to talk."

"That became obvious when the kid said I was her father. What kind of lies have you told her?"

"Lies?" She shoved her chair back and jumped up. "I'll go get Alexandra now, and any obligation I had to contact you will have been fulfilled. I've done my duty. Have a nice life."

He reached for her arm. "Sit down. Please? I'm sorry, but seeing you here with a mini Zann, and hearing her say I'm her father . . ." He lowered his head. "Why would Alexandra say her daddy's name is Kiah Grave? I almost spit out my coffee. I didn't know what to say. She couldn't have made it up. Is that what you told her?"

"Of course not. It's what Zann put on the birth certificate."

"What?! Why would she do that?"

"*Why*? I'll tell you why. She didn't want to write 'illegitimate,' on the line designated for the father. Out of love, she gave her baby a father. Zann used my name when she went to the Home for Unwed Mothers, so my name would be on the certificate. Remember, the Pruitt's were supposed to go to court to adopt *my* baby, since everyone thought I gave birth and my name was on the certificate, but that all changed when Zann died."

"Are you saying they didn't adopt?"

"No. Adoption didn't seem important after we left Pivan Falls and moved to Foggy Bottom, where no one knew us. The whole adoption farce was concocted to protect Zann's reputation. The parson was insistent that the lies cease, so he told his new congregation that his daughter died giving birth and he and Mrs. Pruitt were raising her baby, which of course, was true. Folks thought highly of the preacher, and I'm sure they assumed his daughter was married and her husband was either dead or unable to take on the responsibility of raising a child."

"It's not that I haven't wished many times that she could've been my child. I shouldn't have flown off the handle without waiting for you to explain, but I'm married, now, and my first thought was how my wife might receive such news."

64

He's married?

"We've not been able to have children and she's devastated. If she should hear that I've fathered a child, I can't imagine what it will do to her."

"Believe me, Kiah, I had no idea Alex was going to say that." She feigned a smile. "But I can never second-guess what's coming out of that child's mouth. I came looking for you because Parson Pruitt died and Mrs. Pruitt is terminally insane. I've lived with the Pruitt's as Alex's nursemaid from the day she was born."

Dabney pulled out Zann's letter. "I think you should read this."

His brow's knitted together. "I don't understand. She wrote us both letters before she died and we agreed not to share with one another. Why now?"

"I'd hoped the time would never come, but it has, and I feel an obligation to let you read it."

His lip trembled as he poured over the words. "Oh, Zann, my sweet, sweet Zann. I still have nightmares of not being at the bridge the afternoon she was raped."

"She never blamed you, Kiah. She loved you very much." Dabney gave him a brief summary of her life for the past ten years, and expressed her congratulations to learn he was married. She could only hope she managed to veil her deep disappointment. "Kiah, you were so in love with Zann, I suppose I never suspected you could fall for someone else."

"Oh, Dabs, I never stopped loving Zann. Not for a single day.

My love for her has nothing to do with the love I have for my wife. They're as different as peaches and pomegranates, two of my favorite fruits. Zann was like a sweet, mellow peach and Lizzie . . ." he stopped and grinned. "My Lizzie is more like a pomegranate. Fun and wonderfully tart, once you get past the tough outer shell. She's not at all on the inside the way she sometimes appears on the outside. And just as there are many seeds in a pomegranate, there are many facets to my Lizzie."

"I can tell you love her very much." Dabney fought hard to hide a deep feeling of jealousy. What kind of fruit would he assign to her? Maybe a citron? Nothing to look at on the outside, and not much of value on the inside. Hard to stomach.

"I do love her, Dabs. I love her very much, and I'll do anything to keep her from being hurt. But you were right to honor Zann's request. She knew she could trust you to do the right thing."

"I wasn't sure you'd still be here, but I remembered your father's last name was Lancaster, so I thought I'd start here in Goat Hill and ask around for the Lancaster family."

His face turned red. "That could've been awkward, because my wife would've opened the door. We live at Gladstone. My father died three years ago. I'll need time to prepare Lizzie, but once she understands that Zann was raped and was only thinking of her baby when she had to fill out a birth certificate with a father's name, Alexandra will be welcomed with open arms. Lizzie's crazy about kids."

Dabney's spine stiffened. "Let me be clear, Kiah. I didn't bring Alex here to put her off on you. She's like my own child. I plan to raise her. However, I felt a moral responsibility to notify you since Zann was specific in requesting you be contacted if anything happened to her parents. I'm glad you walked in when you did, because now that we've talked, I've fulfilled my duty. When Alex comes back, we can leave."

Kiah glared. "Leave? Dabney, you can't leave with her."

Her eyes squinted. "What do you mean, I *can't* leave with her?"

"Forgive me, I didn't mean I was forbidding you. I simply meant I want to get to know her. Zann would want that, don't you think?"

"Sorry. I suppose we're both a little on edge. And you're right. Zann would want you to have an opportunity to get to know her daughter."

"So you'll stay?"

Dabney nodded. "I saw a motel as I drove into town. We'll stay there tonight. I have three-and-a-half weeks left before having to vacate the parsonage. I need to look for a job and a permanent place to stay. I moved with the Pruitts from Pivan Falls, years ago and I've enjoyed living in Foggy Bottom. The people are wonderful, but there are no jobs there."

"What kind of work are you looking for?"

"I'll do anything that'll allow me to keep Alex nearby." She felt a blush rise to the top of her head and quickly added, "I didn't mean *anything*." Was he recalling the nasty high school gossip by all the pimple-faced braggarts? Plunging ahead, she said, "Maybe a waitress, where Alexandra can come to the restaurant after school, or a housekeeper, preferably with a family who has children and wouldn't mind her coming to work with me."

"Well, I know of a woman here in Goat Hill who's looking for a housekeeper-cook, but she's an ornery old soul and doesn't have young children."

"Then I'm sure she wouldn't want a ten-year-old roaming around the house."

"That shouldn't be a problem, since she has maid's quarters back of the big house. Alexandra would be close by at all times. It'd be perfect. Would you like me to call her?"

"I do need a job and it won't be easy finding one. Would you mind?"

"Not at all. I'll call her now."

He walked outside to the payphone, then returned to the table smiling. "I think the job's yours if you want it. She sounded quite pleased, especially after the glowing recommendation I gave you. Here's the address. Her name's Mrs. Lula Weinberger and she wants to interview you in the morning at ten o'clock. I have a feeling it's simply a formality. She needs a maid and needs one now. I doubt the woman knows which end of a broom to use to sweep the floor."

"You said she didn't have young children. Older children?"

"One. An overgrown kid who still lives at home. Oliver's

twenty-seven, but a real mama's boy. The elder Mr. Weinberger died years ago, and Oliver's mother keeps her boy under her thumb." Kiah chuckled, as if he'd just had a funny thought. "She buys all of his clothes and still dresses him like Little Lord Fauntleroy. He's not much of a man in my opinion, to let his mama run his life the way she does."

"That's sad."

"You're still a softy. You'll see what I mean when you see him. A real milksop."

"Maybe I am a softy, Kiah, but I remember what it's like to be labeled."

"You're right. I shouldn't have said that. But what am I supposed to tell the kid? She'll find out who I am and she thinks I'm her father."

"I don't know, Kiah. We'll play it by ear. I don't want to lie to her, but neither do I want her to know the horrid truth. I know that together we'll figure it out."

Dabney looked up and saw Alexandra waiting to cross the street. "Here she comes."

He jumped up and threw money on the table. "I'd like to pay for your lunch, but I have to be gone before Alex walks in. I need time to sort things out. It was great seeing you again, Dabney. I'll keep in touch. I'm sure you'll get the job."

And he was gone.

Chapter Nine

Dabney held tightly to Alexandra's hand as they walked up the tall marble steps of the Weinberger mansion. She rang the doorbell.

"Is this a castle?" Alex whispered.

Dabney put her finger to her lips and shushed her. As she waited, erratic thoughts flitted through her head like an LP record played at fast speed. For years, Dabney had dreamed of one day finding Kiah, but the long-held fantasy of the two of them getting together came to a halt when she spotted a gold band on his third finger, left hand. A sudden throbbing headache caused her to rethink the crazy decision to stay in the same town, knowing she'd die a little each time she ran into him. Hadn't she fulfilled her obligation? She'd found Kiah and he'd seen Alexandra. Wasn't that all that was required of her? "Alex, maybe we shouldn't—"

Before she could finish her sentence, a tall, slender man wearing wire-rimmed glasses, a top-coat and ruffled shirt opened the door. "Good morning, ladies. To what do I owe this pleasure?"

Dabney was relieved that he opened the door when he did, before she had a chance to leave. She needed a job. After all, she had a child to provide for. "Good morning, sir." She licked her dry lips and made an attempt to steady her voice. "I'm Dabney Foxworthy and I'm here to interview for the position of housekeeper."

Seconds seemed like minutes when he continued to stare without responding. Dabney shifted on her feet. "Uh . . . and this is my ward, Alexandra."

The spunky ten-year-old stepped forward and extended her hand. "Call me Alex."

As usual, Alexandra had managed to break the ice.

He bent down, took her hand, raised it to his lips and kissed it "Pleased to make your acquaintance Miss Alex. My name is Oliver. Please come in and I'll let my mother know you're here."

"Are you a butler?"

Dabney grimaced. If only she'd told Alexandra to wait in the car. This was too important to mess up.

The corner of his mouth lifted in a slight smile. "Not the butler. I live here."

"You look like a butler. Not that I've ever seen one, but I thought that's how they dressed."

Dabney felt a hot blush rise to her face. "I'm so sorry."

"No need for apologies. I hope you get the job. I think Alex and I could get along quite well. She's delightful. Please be seated in the parlor while I inform my mother that you've arrived."

Alex roamed the room with her eyes. "Will we live here if you get the job?"

"Shh! I hear someone coming. Let me do the talking, Alexandra."

A short, stout lady, with gray hair in finger waves, peered over the top of her spectacles. "My son tells me you're the young lady Hezekiah recommended."

Relieved that the woman hadn't called him Kiah, she said, "Yes ma'am. I'm Dabney Foxworthy. I appreciate the opportunity to interview for the position." Dabney withdrew her hand, when Lula refused to accept it.

"According to Hezekiah, you've had years of experience as a housekeeper."

"Yes ma'am. Eleven, to be exact."

"Can you cook?"

Alex blurted, "She's a great cook. She can cook anything, can't you, Dabs?"

Dabney's shoulders fell, seeing the stern expression on the woman's face.

The woman's gaze went from the top of Alexandra's head to the soles on her shoes, before she responded. "Well, I don't usually consider hiring anyone with children, but you come highly recommended. So you can occupy the maid's quarters out back. If the child needs you during the day, she can come to the back door and state her business, and you'll be allowed to check on her in between duties. I must warn you, though, I can't have her running wild inside my house. There's too many things she could break. I think you'll find the quarters quite comfortable. There's a phone. However, if you choose to abuse it by making long distance calls, I'll be forced to have it removed. It's there for my convenience, not yours. Should I need you in the middle of the night, I'd like to be able to call you."

"You mean . . ."

"Yes, you have the job. I'd like you to start as soon as possible. You'll have Sundays and Thursday afternoons off. Oliver and I eat at the club on Sundays, and I'll expect you to have Thursday's evening meal prepared before you leave at noon. The cottage isn't furnished. Do you have furniture?"

"Yes ma'am. We'll drive back to Foggy Bottom, pack our things and I'll find someone to move us, Saturday, and be ready to start first thing Monday morning."

Oliver stood leaning against the door jam. "I have a new truck. I'll be happy to move you."

His mother's brows knitted together. "I'm sure she appreciates the offer, Oliver, but that won't be possible. You have duties with your law practice and no time for such. With the nation in a Depression, finding a laborer willing to make a few dollars shouldn't be a problem."

Dabney nodded. "Your offer was very kind, sir, but your mother's right. I'm sure I can find someone to move us."

****

Thursday morning, two men from Parson Pruitt's congregation

unloaded the last piece of furniture and Dabney walked into her new home. The cottage was small, but adequate.

She enrolled Alexandra in her new school, then walked back to the car and squalled. "Lord, I thank you for the job, and a place to live, but it was so hard to leave Alex just now, in a classroom full of strangers. Please help her to adjust to this new life. She's been through so much and although she seems to ride the waves, I sometimes look into those big eyes and wonder what's going on behind them. I'm afraid I won't be able to spend as much time with her as I'd like. Please, Lord, send my little Alex a friend."

Mrs. Weinberger spent the morning giving Dabney a tour of the house and gardens, along with all the instructions of duties she was expected to perform.

Dabney put on the white uniform and kept her eye on the clock as she worked, eager for three o'clock to come, when the school bus would be bringing Alex back.

At twelve o'clock, she approached Mrs. Weinberger. "Ma'am, dinner's ready."

Peering over the top of her spectacles, she huffed. "Young lady, is that how your former employers allowed you to announce the meals? Hezekiah led me to believe you were experienced. Dinner is in the evening, not midday. Lunch is at noon. And you should say, 'Lunch is served, madam. Not lunch is ready. Understand?'"

"Sorry ma'am. The Pruitts had breakfast, dinner and supper,

not breakfast lunch and dinner. I'll try again." She cleared her throat. "Lunch is served, ma'am."

"Much better. Now, I think you'll find my son in his office down the hall. Please inform him of the same."

Dabney stood at the open door. "Mr. Weinberger, lunch is served. Sir."

"Thank you, Dabney."

Oliver appeared very impressed with the meal, though his mother had little to say. Dabney considered that to be a good sign, since she was confident if the woman hadn't liked it, she would've been quick to let her know.

She hurried to finish up in the kitchen and get dinner started, so she'd have a few minutes to spend when Alex arrived home from school. She watched from the window. Her heart pounded when the bus rounded the corner. Her eyes widened, then blinked several times, unable to believe what she was seeing. Oliver stood at the curb, waiting for the bus door to open. Alex jumped off, grabbed his hand as if it were their custom. She appeared to be full of talk as he walked her toward the back of the house.

Dabney approached Mrs. Weinberger in the library. "Excuse me, ma'am, but Alexandra is home from school. Would it be permissible for me to spend a few minutes with her? Being it was her first day, I'm sure she . . ."

Without looking up from her book, Lula waved her hand. "Shoo. I told you if you had your chores done, you could check on the child from time to time. I'm not an ogre, you know. Do what you have to do. Just make certain you don't shirk your responsibilities as a servant."

"Yes ma'am." She jerked off her apron and hung it up, then hurried out the kitchen door. She smiled seeing Oliver and Alex sitting in a glider on the small front porch of the cottage. She couldn't tell which one seemed to be enjoying it the most. "Thank you, Lord," she whispered. "Actually, I had a child in mind when I prayed for Alex to have a friend, but maybe Kiah was right and Oliver is just an overgrown kid."

Oliver stood when Dabney approached. "That was a wonderful lunch you prepared. I don't know when I've enjoyed anything as much."

Alex said "Didn't I tell you she was a good cook? She can make anything."

"Thank you, Mr. Weinberger. I appreciate those kind words."

"Please, call me Oliver."

She shook her head and the corner of her mouth twitched in a smile. "I'm not sure your mother would approve."

"I'll handle mother. I prefer Oliver to Mr. Weinberger."

"Then Oliver it is. Excuse me while I prepare a snack for Alexandra. And thank you for meeting her at the bus stop. That was kind of you."

"My pleasure. She's a charming young lady. We've had a very informative conversation."

Dabney dared not ask.

76

Chapter Ten

Dabney wiped sweat from her brow and glanced back up at the large clock above the stove. A quarter past five. Holding a dishrag in her hand, she opened the oven door and gently squeezed a sweet potato, only to discover it was almost as hard as when she placed them in the oven.

Never had it taken so long to bake sweet potatoes. Mrs. Weinberger had been very specific in saying dinner was to be served at precisely six o'clock, not a minute before, not a minute after. What if the potatoes weren't ready in time? If they didn't soften soon, she'd simply slice them and quick fry them in butter and brown sugar. Had she put too much salt in the beans? What if Mrs. Weinberger couldn't eat salt?

Seemed she looked for things to worry about, lately. It wasn't as if there weren't plenty of real problems requiring her attention without adding the what-ifs. The potatoes were done in plenty of time, the roast was tender, the beans seasoned perfectly. And when

Mrs. Weinberger's only complaint was that the onions in the salad should've been sliced instead of chopped, Dabney let out a sigh of relief.

After cleaning the kitchen, she turned out the light and walked out the back door. Her lip held a gentle curl, seeing Oliver and Alexandra chasing lightening bugs in front of the cottage and placing them in a Mason jar. "What are you doing out here, Mr. Weinbur . . .Oliver?"

"Chasing fireflies, of course!" He chuckled as if he were truly enjoying himself.

"He's funny, Dabs. And you know what? He knows my daddy."

Dabney grabbed hold of the porch rail when her knees weakened. "Oh, Alexandra, honey, you have it all wrong. You know I asked you not to . . ."

Oliver held up his palm. "No need to scold her. Alex and I are buddies. Her secret is safe with me. I've told her a few of my own."

Alexandra confirmed it with a nod. "Yeah, Oliver said one time he. . ." She popped her hand over her mouth. "Oops! Sorry, Oliver. I won't tell. Promise!"

Dabney's pulse raced. "Alexandra, you go inside and start working on your homework. I'll be in shortly. I'd like to speak with Oliver for a moment."

He said, "It's a nice night for a stroll. Why don't we take a short walk through the gardens, and you tell me what's on your mind."

They walked down a long path before either of them spoke.

Oliver led her under an arbor, and down another trail. He finally said, "What's on your mind?"

"If you know Kiah Grave, then I'm sure you have a good idea what's on my mind, Oliver. Alex doesn't know what she's talking about. Kiah is *not* her father."

"Oh? Then, who is her father?"

"That I can't tell you."

"Do you know?"

His question irritated her, though she wasn't sure why. It was a logical question. "Oliver, please don't ask me to divulge any information concerning Alexandra's parentage. She isn't the one hired to work here and therefore I see no reason to give an account of her heritage."

"Sorry! I can see I've upset you. I meant no harm."

"No, I should apologize. I shouldn't have become so defensive. It's just that Alex is quite the romantic. She's never met her real father, and when she heard Kiah was her mother's boyfriend in high school, she made these false assumptions."

"She claims his name is on the birth certificate. You're saying that's a false assumption?" He threw up his hands. "Oops. There I go again. No more questions. If I seemed more than a little curious, it's because I was taken aback at Alex's unsolicited announcement, proclaiming herself to be Kiah's daughter. That was quite a shocker."

Dabney stopped, and leaned over to smell a rose. "Ah, I love roses."

Oliver pulled out a pocket knife, snipped the rose and stuck it in her hair. "Dabney, since Mother said Kiah is the one who recommended you, I suppose you and he are . . ."

"Friends! Nothing more."

"That's good."

She laughed. "Did you really think I came here to have a rendezvous with Kiah Grave? He's a married man, you know."

"Yes, I'm fully aware. I was once engaged to the woman he married."

The information caught Dabney off guard. "You? And the girl he married?"

"I can understand why that shocks you that the same woman who would fall for Kiah could've once been engaged to me."

Dabney's foot went so far in her mouth she wasn't sure she could ever pull it back out. Regardless of how hard she attempted to smooth over her words, the hurt look on Oliver's face confirmed that he'd correctly read her thoughts.

"I can see I've embarrassed you, Dabney. That wasn't my intent. The truth is, Eliza never loved me. I was crazy about her for all the wrong reasons, and I knew how she loathed me. She proposed to me, not because she loved me, but to make Kiah jealous. Then, when he left town, she was angry that her little plan didn't work and she broke our engagement and left for college. She stayed gone for seven years, and to show you how dumb I am, I held on to the idiotic notion that we'd one day tie the knot. I thought marrying Eliza would miraculously change my persona. But to her I was still Armadillo Face and always will be."

"Armadillo Face? I don't understand."

"That was her pet name for me in sixth grade. Mother tried to console me and make me think it was a term of endearment, but I knew better. To the other kids at school, I was Fauntleroy. They claimed—and rightly so—that I looked like Little Lord Fauntleroy because Mother dressed me in knickers, long after the other fellows were sporting long pants."

"Oh, Oliver, that must've been very painful for you."

"For sure, it wasn't the person I wanted to be, but I knew it was who I was. Even I couldn't deny the comparison."

From the drawn lines on his forehead, Dabney had a feeling the raw pain was still as fresh as sixth grade. Hoping to turn the conversation toward a more favorable memory, she said, "What was your favorite pastime when you were a child?"

"That's easy. I enjoyed watching the other boys play football every Saturday afternoon in the cow pasture across from the church. I wanted to play so bad I could taste it, but Mother would've taken a strap to me. She claimed the game was barbaric, and she didn't want me skinning my knees and messing up my knickers." He stopped and gave a hollow chuckle, though it had a sad ring to it. "I came home one day and took the scissors and cut up every pair of knickers in my closet, then stuffed them all under the bed."

"Kids can be cruel. I'm so sorry. What did your mother do?"

"I got a tongue lashing, then she went to Blumberg's and bought me a half-dozen new pair. But the worse part was when she went to the school and demanded the teacher give a lecture on name-calling."

"Did that stop it?"

"What do you think?"

Dabney shook her head. "It didn't work."

"You're right. It only made things worse. The name Fauntleroy stuck all through high school, and even to this day, I'm often addressed as Fauntleroy." He reached up and swiped his brow with his hand. "Gee, I don't know why I'm going off at the mouth like this. I've been with you ten minutes and already I've shared more of my heart with you than I have with anyone else in all my twenty-seven years. I guess we'd better walk back to the cottage, before I really make an idiot of myself."

"You're no idiot, Oliver, but I should get back. Alexandra will be wondering where we went."

"Dabney, thank you."

"For what?"

"For listening. It feels good to talk to someone who listens."

"You're an interesting person, Oliver. I've enjoyed our talk."

He walked her to the door, and she heard him whistling as he headed back to the big house.

She thought of the name Kiah called him in the cafe. Milksop. Well, maybe on the outside he did look like a genuine milksop, but that's not who he was on the inside. On the inside, he was a deep thinker—a very compassionate man. He just needed someone other than his mother to help him match his outsides to his insides.

Chapter Eleven

Dabney had just put Alex to bed when the telephone rang. Hearing Kiah's voice on the other end caused her heart to flutter like a school girl's. She had to get him out of her mind. And she would. *He's married.* But cutting him out of her heart would take some time.

Seeing him again had brought back all the old feelings. Not that he ever had any for her, but never had she loved anyone the way she loved that man.

"Hi, Dabs. I told my wife that a friend from my youth was in town, and she insisted I invite you and Alexandra to go to church with us Sunday, then have lunch with us afterward."

"Oh, Kiah, I'm not sure that's a good idea."

"Sure, it is. I want Lizzie to get to know you both, and for you to know her. You'll see for yourself why I fell in love with my beautiful wife, even though she's nothing at all like Zann."

Her heart felt as if shards of glass were piercing it from every side. "I'm sure she's a wonderful person, but I can't be responsible for what Alexandra might say. She's so enamored with the thought of Kiah Grave being her father and though I promised her grandfather I wouldn't lie to her, I can't bring myself to tell her the horrid truth."

"Don't worry about it. I'll explain the situation to Lizzie. It won't be a problem. I've missed you, Dabney. I'm thrilled that you're staying here in Goat Hill. So . . . Sunday, then? We'll pick you and the kid up around ten-forty-five. Church begins at eleven."

Against her better judgment she agreed.

Alex rolled over in bed. "Who were you talking to?"

"I thought you were asleep." Dabney sighed. Why put off the inevitable? "That was Kiah Grave on the phone."

She squealed. "My daddy? How did he know where to find me? Where is he? I want to meet him. Will you take me to him, Dabney? Will you, please?"

After calming her, Dabney explained the man she saw in the diner was Kiah Grave, but there were unusual circumstances surrounding her birth, which could prove hurtful to some people if shared at the wrong time. "You have to trust me, Alex. One day, when you're older, I'll answer all the questions you have. But for now, please don't mention to anyone else that you believe Kiah to be your father."

"But he is."

"Please, Alexandra? For his sake."

"Oh, I get it. Because after my mama died, he probably

85

married someone else, and his wife might be jealous of my mama, especially if she finds out they had a baby."

Dabney rolled those words around in her head. Perfect. She'd go with it. "Yes, he's married, and I suppose his wife has probably heard that your mother and Kiah were sweethearts in high school. So if you were to blurt out that he's your father, I suspect it could cause a stressful situation in his marriage. For his sake, do you think you can forget that idea for a while and not mention it again?"

"Sure, Dabs. Not that I can ever forget, but I'll keep my mouth shut because I wouldn't want to hurt my daddy. He's swell. As long as he and I both know the truth, no one else has to know."

Dabney blew out a heavy breath. "Good girl."

****

Dabney liked her new job, and Alexandra appeared to be adjusting much better than she'd expected, thanks to Oliver spending so much time with her. Mrs. Weinberger wasn't the easiest person to get along with, but Dabney did her best to keep her happy.

Even though the house was huge, there were many spare rooms that no one ever entered, so it didn't take long to run a dust mop and feather-dust those areas. Sometimes she pretended it was her beautiful home, which made cleaning fun. The huge kitchen had a pantry with shelves reaching from the floor to the ceiling, packed with all sorts of canned goods. Huge hams hung from hooks in the smokehouse, located directly behind the cottage. Even in her dreams, she'd never seen so much food.

Dabney wondered how she might've turned out if she'd been born in such luxury instead of growing up in a Rooster Run shanty with a mother who drank herself to death.

Thursday morning, she sent Alex off to school on the bus and busied herself in the kitchen, preparing breakfast, lunch and dinner all at the same time. For breakfast, she baked a baker of biscuits, scrambled eggs, fried a slab of ham and made red-eye gravy. She cut up a chicken, floured it and left it in the pan in the Frigidaire, ready to fry for lunch. She'd made the potato salad the night before and the butterbeans were cooking on the back eye. As soon as the biscuits were done, she'd slide in the pot roast and vegetables, so everything would be finished cooking before she left for her afternoon off.

After serving Mrs. Weinberger and Oliver breakfast, she sat down at the small porcelain table in the kitchen with a cup of coffee and a cold biscuit.

The morning went fast and Dabney supposed it was because she had so much to do to keep her busy. She finished in the kitchen at 12:30 and walked over to the cottage. She gathered up a few dirty clothes, washed them in the sink, then hung them on the line to dry in the sunshine. A few dogwood trees in the distance were beginning to bloom, even though it was a little early. Spring was her favorite season when the woods looked like one giant bouquet with wild azaleas, wisteria, Carolina jasmine, honeysuckle and flowering fruit trees all in bloom.

After hanging clothes, Leo, the gardener waved and hollered, "A good day to you, Miz Dabney. Enjoying this beautiful weather, are ya?" Pruning roses in the Browning section of the garden, he explained Mrs. Weinberger named each section after famous poets.

"I certainly am. The garden looks beautiful. You've done a great job."

"I thank you, kindly. It's my belief we should all bloom where God plants us, and that's what these roses and I intend to do. Have you noticed, Miz Dabney, that even wild blooms, which people refer to as weeds are often quite beautiful in their own right? Take the dandelion. Adults yank it up by the roots and try to kill it, yet it amuses children. They find joy in chasing it as it blows in the wind. It has its place. Yes ma'am, God made the flowers, but He also made the weeds. Weeds are strong and push through the dirt and refuse to give up easily. Weeds survive harsh treatment and aren't destroyed by opinions. You ever seen dollar weed shrivel up and disappear, just because people badmouth it? No ma'am, it stands its ground. Admirable qualities, I'd say. And who's to say dollar weed ain't as pretty as some of these fancy grasses sold in the nurseries? I ask you, Miz Dabney—who gets to decide which plants are respectable and which ones are to be done away with?"

"That's a good question, Leo."

"Yes'm. I think so, too. But I reckon I need to get back to work, less Mrs. Weinberger comes and catches me dawdling. Though she insists I kill all weeds, I talk to 'em and let 'em know I admire their tenacity, and I expect them to come back, fighting for their space." He chuckled. "And you know what? They listen to me. Just between the two of us, I think it's because they know if they didn't keep coming back, I'd be out of a job."

Dabney walked over to the Frost garden, sat on the concrete bench and inhaled the wonderful fragrance. She mulled over Leo's words. She gathered from his accent he was not born in America, and she had a feeling his life had not been an easy one. Yet, his countenance was as sweet and lovely as any flower in the garden. His were not idle words. He did indeed bloom where he was planted. For too long, Dabney had felt like a weed. Worthless. She'd allowed her past to destroy her before she had a chance to bloom. Not anymore. So what if she wasn't a rose. Maybe she was a dandelion. But Leo was right. God made both, the rose and the dandelion. If Leo could bloom where he was planted, she could too. And she would. Lost in her thoughts, she failed to see Oliver approaching.

"May I join you?"

"Please do."

"Resting? I'm sure you're exhausted. The lunch was wonderful. I don't know what you did to the chicken, but it was the best fried chicken I've ever put in my mouth."

She giggled. "You're making me blush. It was nothing special."

"Not true. I think everything you do is very special."

Caught by surprise at his statement, she quickly changed the subject. "Look, is that a mockingbird?"

Without taking his eyes off her, he mumbled. "I believe it is."

She smiled. "You didn't look."

"I looked with my ears. It's a mockingbird."

"Oliver, I don't think . . . well, it just doesn't seem—Nevermind."

"Dabney, I see I've embarrassed you. I'm sorry. That wasn't my intent."

Exactly what was his intent? Had she read too much in his comment? He was a wealthy socialite. He was an attorney. He'd inherited a huge textile mill, which employed eighty percent of the population in the Wiregrass area. Oliver Weinberger was *somebody*.

She was a housekeeper. Daughter of a prostitute and an unknown father. A *nobody*. How presumptuous of her to suspect his words were anything more than an act of kindness. He merely said everything she did was special. What made her think he referred to anything other than the way she cooked and cleaned house?

Relieved that she didn't embarrass herself further by letting him know she initially misunderstood his intentions, she mumbled, "I appreciate the compliment, Oliver. Really, I do. Not being accustomed to receiving many, I haven't had much practice in knowing how to accept them graciously." Seeing the puzzled look on his face caused her to suspect he now must think her a nincompoop. She jumped up. "What am I doing sitting here? I have loads to do. Have a good day, Oliver." And she scurried off to the cottage, without allowing him time to respond.

Chapter Twelve

Oliver rolled over and switched on the lamp. Three a.m. and his eyes hadn't closed all night. He sat up on the edge of the bed with his elbows propped on his knees, his face buried in his hands. The huge grandfather clock downstairs struck four.

"She's laughing behind my back and I have no one to blame but myself. First, I whine about being called Fauntleroy in school, which served only to confirm her opinion of me, then I drool like a hungry dog, while gushing over her." What made him tell her things he'd struggled years to forget? "I suppose she got a real kick out of the story of me and my knickers. That bit of information should be fit fodder to liven up a dull party." At the taste of hot bile, he stood, grabbed his robe from the bedpost and walked into the bathroom, searching for something to combat the nausea.

"Oliver? Is that you, dear?"

"Yes ma'am."

"What's wrong? Are you sick, sugar?"

"I'm fine. Go back to sleep, mother."

He opened the medicine cabinet and reached for a box of sodium bicarbonate. He closed the mirrored door and groaned at the milksop looking back at him. Nothing in his life would ever change. He couldn't blame others for correctly identifying him. He'd always be Fauntleroy, living with his controlling mother. The only friends he'd ever have would be tied to his money. Squeezing the soda box in his hand, he slowly poured the contents into the toilet. What good was a temporary fix? Sure, money could buy him a wife, but it couldn't buy love. He'd gladly give it all away for Dabney Foxworthy's love. But the qualities he'd admired most about her were the same qualities that separated them.

Oliver spotted an aspirin tin lying beside the sink. Strange, he hadn't noticed it before now. Maybe it was a sign. He'd prayed for the pain to go away. Was this his answer? He popped it open and stood staring at the white round pills. A sure way out of a life not worth living. His throat swelled. *I'm not even man enough to do it.* He opened the medicine cabinet, deposited the tin box on the top shelf and sobbed.

****

It became evident to Dabney in the following days that Oliver purposely avoided her, which troubled her greatly. Even when she served the meals, his demeanor was changed. Though he remained polite, his words were cool and generic. Instead of raving about the delicious food, he merely folded his napkin and said, "I enjoyed the meal. Thank you." He continued to wait at the curb for Alex to get off the bus and walked her to the cottage, yet he never lingered. Before Dabney could hang up her apron and scoot out the back door, he was gone. *He knew I misinterpreted his kindness in the garden as something more meaningful, and now he's afraid to even talk to me.*

But Oliver wasn't her only concern. Sunday was coming and the thought of being with Kiah and his uppity wife sent shivers down her spine. She supposed since Kiah inherited his father's estate, he was now a big shot in Goat Hill. No doubt his wife had heard all about how Dabney begged Kiah to take her with him when he left Pivan Falls ten years ago, even though she knew he didn't love her. The image of her throwing herself at him, pleading for him to marry her, brought tears to her eyes. How could she face his wife?

Leo's words came back to her. So, what if she *was* a weed. Weeds have their place. Why was it so hard for her to remember her place on this earth? Could it be because just once in her lifetime she'd like to know what it feels like to be a rose? Was that so wrong?

Mrs. Weinberger's wash woman, Lettie, came twice a week, on Wednesdays and Saturdays. Her little girl, Nelda Sue—or Nelsue, as her mama called her—was in Alexandra's classroom at school, so the two little girls rode the bus together on Wednesday afternoons and the child came with her mother on Saturdays. Dabney was glad, since Saturday would've been lonesome for Alex, and the girls played well together.

When Lettie made preparations to leave Saturday evening, she invited Alex to go home with Nelda Sue for a sleep-over, promising she'd have her back by Sunday afternoon. The offer couldn't have come at a more perfect time, since Dabney dreaded taking Alex with her Sunday morning, not knowing what might pop out of the child's mouth.

"No! I can't go." Alex balked. "We're going to church with Kiah Grave tomorrow."

In spite of Dabney's efforts to encourage the sleep-over, Alex remained adamant.

Nelda Sue ran to the car squalling, as Lettie tried to smooth things over. "Don't worry, Dabney. Nelsue's disappointed, but she'll get over it. Maybe another time. Is Mr. Grave a relative or a family friend?"

Dabney mumbled, "Kiah's an old friend from years back."

Lettie's mouth separated in a grin. "Did I see a twinkle in your eye, Dabney Foxworthy? An old boyfriend, by chance?"

Before she could decide how to answer, Alex broke in. "No, they were just friends. He's my . . ." She stopped and looked wide-eyed at Dabney. "He's nice."

Chapter Thirteen

Sunday morning Dabney went over a slew of instructions with Alexandra, though she could've summed it all up in five words. Be seen and not heard.

Dabney had never believed in stifling Alex's need to express herself, but she reminded her that to go into Kiah's home and even hint he was her father could destroy his marriage, which would be very hurtful and unfair to him. Alex assured her she understood. But did she, really? Dabney had long ago learned not to be surprised at what unexpected verbiage might spill from the ten-year-old kid's unstoppable mouth.

At precisely ten-forty-five, Kiah and his wife drove up in front of the cottage. Kiah jumped out and opened the back door to the vehicle. After the introductions and initial polite chit-chat, the ride became very quiet. And very long. Or so it seemed.

The woman was beautiful with peaches and cream complexion and hair the color of corn silk. With class written all over her, she carried herself like a queen. From this quick observation, Dabney gathered Eliza Grave grew up with wealth and didn't marry Kiah for the money he inherited. She couldn't help wonder if his wife would've fallen in love with him when he was dirt poor. *I loved him for who he was, not for what he had, for he had nothing.* She clinched her eyes shut and tried to blot out the memory that felt a bit adulterous. Kiah Grave was a married man and she had no business dredging up old feelings. For ten years, he'd been nothing more than a fantasy, but a fantasy that must now end.

****

Oliver stood at his upstairs window, which overlooked the gardens and the cottage. He had a nauseated feeling, seeing Kiah Grave's car pull up and Dabney and Alexandra waiting to get in. He couldn't see Eliza, though he was sure she was sitting in the front seat. With Kiah Grave's masculine looks, the lucky fellow could've landed any girl he wanted, with or without his wealth.

In keeping with Oliver's luck in love, the two women sitting in Kiah's car happened to be the only two women for whom Oliver had ever shown an interest. He realized now that although he pined after Eliza throughout high school and into college, he was never really in love with her. His infatuation was nothing more than childish rebellion. She epitomized everything his mother hated. As far as Lula Weinberger was concerned, the only thing Eliza had going for her was the fact she was Will Lancaster's daughter. But Eliza's fun-loving attitude and daring escapades caused Oliver's mother much consternation.

97

He watched out the upstairs window as Kiah opened the car door and Dabney slid in. Oliver had never seen her looking so beautiful. The dress wasn't fancy, but she would've looked good in a guano sack. Alexandra wore a sundress, her hair platted in pigtails, and as usual, she was all giggly. Funny how a ten-year-old could've wrapped herself around his heart in such a short time.

The doorknob twisted and he whirled around at the sound of his mother's voice. She beat on the door and yelled. "Oliver Weinberger, how many times have I told you not to lock this door? What if you should get deathly ill in the middle of the night and I couldn't get to you? What do you suppose would happen then?"

"I'd die in peace?"

"Oliver! Unlock it this instant."

Like the puppet he was, he trudged over and opened the door.

"Oliver, darling, put on your pinstriped suit and that paisley tie I bought you last week and hurry or we'll be late for church."

"Yes, mother."

****

The church was larger than the ones Mack pastored back in Pivan Falls and Foggy Bottom, but the people were exceptionally friendly. Eliza took it upon herself to make the introductions, and Dabney didn't correct her when she was introduced as someone from Kiah's hometown, who moved to Goat Hill in response to Lula Weinberger's need for a housekeeper.

Eliza ended the introductions by wrapping her arms around Alex and gushing, "And this beautiful child is Alexandra." Dabney stiffened. Eliza apparently thought the child was hers. After worrying for four days Kiah might've told his wife too much, Dabney spent the last four minutes wondering why he would've said so little.

After church they drove to a downtown restaurant. The awkward silence at the table was deafening. Dabney had begun to regret asking Alex to keep quiet, since the kid was so good at breaking the ice in a tense situation, and the ice in the dining room was so thick, one could skate on it.

Dabney could feel Kiah's concern that Alex might drop the bombshell and that could account for his tied tongue. Never had she seen him so quiet.

Eliza broke the silence. "So, Dabney, Kiah tells me you and he were neighbors when you were children. What was he like as a little boy?"

She glanced at Kiah. "Nice."

Eliza laughed. "Is that all you remember about him? That he was nice? I'll bet the girls were all crazy about him, weren't they?"

Dabney forced a smile. "He was quite studious and didn't pay a lot of attention to girls."

Alex pulled on Dabney's sleeve. "What about my mama?" Then as if she'd seen a ghost, Alexandra quickly covered her face with both hands. "I'm sorry. I'm sorry, Kiah. It slipped."

Eliza turned and glared at her husband. "What slipped? What is she talking about?"

Seeing the shock on Eliza's face, Alexandra shoved her chair

99

back, and ran out of the restaurant sobbing. Dabney ran after her, and after catching her, she sat down on a bench and held the distraught child in her arms. "It's okay, honey. Don't worry."

"But he's gonna hate me."

"No, he's not and neither am I." Dabney looked up to see Kiah and Eliza standing there.

Eliza knelt beside Alex and said, "You did nothing wrong, sweetheart. I overreacted because I thought . . . well, it doesn't matter what I thought. Why don't we go to my house, sit down with ice cream and cake and we'll let everything come out in the open."

Confused, Alexandra glanced at Dabney for instructions, but Dabney had none to give. "Everything?" she asked.

Eliza took a handkerchief from her purse and dried Alex's tears. "Everything. I hate secrets, don't you?"

Alexandra smiled through the tears and nodded. "Yes ma'am, because I'm not very good at keeping them."

Kiah stepped up. "I hate to be the bearer of bad news, but I'm afraid we need to postpone our little ice cream party for another day. I need to run over to the cotton gin and take a look at the equipment. Felix told me at church this morning they checked the arms on the vacuum yesterday, and it appears we may need to make a replacement."

Eliza's brow shot up. "Today? Why is it necessary that you go today, when cotton won't be ready to gin for months?"

"I have to order the parts, Eliza, and have it installed. I may

100

need a whole new system. I'm sorry, but Felix is planning to meet me at the gin in thirty minutes. I didn't realize you'd planned an ice cream party afterward. I told him I could meet him there at one-thirty. Dabney, I do apologize. I'm glad you and Alexandra were able to go with us to church. I enjoyed having lunch with you. We'll have to do this again and next time, I'll make sure I allow for a nice long visit afterward."

Driving them back to the cottage, Eliza and Kiah said little more than a few words to one another.

****

Kiah sat in his easy chair Sunday evening, reading the paper.

"Sweetheart?" Lizzie's brow furrowed.

He lowered the paper and looked over the top. "What's wrong, Lizzie?"

"Wrong? Did I say something was wrong?"

"No, but I know you. You've been moody ever since I came back from the gin. What's troubling you?"

"I wouldn't say it's troubling, exactly."

"Then exactly what would you call it?"

"Curiosity, maybe?"

"Well, I'll forget calling the doctor, because if that's all that ails you, I'd say you're acting normal. It's your nature to be curious." He turned to the Sports page and continued to read.

****

Alexandra crossed her arms over her chest. "Well, I ruined a good day, didn't I?"

101

Dabney wrapped her arms around her. "No, sweetie. You didn't ruin a thing. In fact, I had a very nice time, didn't you?"

She formed a pout and went to her room.

Dabney sensed this day had not gone as Alex had hoped, but all changed when Lettie and her little girl drove up at three o'clock.

Nelda Sue jumped out and ran through the cottage to Alex's room.

Lettie said, "I Suwannee, Nelsue has moped around all morning, and I promised her we'd come see if Alexandra was back. I realize it's a school night, but if she's willing, would you mind her going home with us for a sleep-over with Nelsue? I'll see to it that they're in bed by nine o'clock, and they can catch the bus together in the morning."

"Lettie, you're a God-send. Alex has had a bad day, and I think this is a wonderful idea."

"Oh, I'm sorry to hear that. I don't mean to be nosey, but you look as if yours wasn't much better. Of course, when our kids hurt, we hurt. I'm a good listener if you'd like to talk about it."

Dabney smiled. "No, it's not my place. Just suffice it to say, my little Alex sometimes gets carried away with fantasies and when they don't materialize, she becomes devastated. It never lasts very long, but it breaks my heart to see her hurting, even for a short while."

The two girls came walking outside and Alex was all smiles. "Can I Dabney? Can I sleep over?"

"Can you be good?"

"I promise."

"Then I see no reason not to let you. Go pack your school clothes, your pajamas and toothbrush. And don't forget your books and homework."

Nelda Sue giggled. "She's packed them already."

Dabney felt a tug on her heartstrings, watching them drive away. It was the first night she'd ever allowed her to spend the night away from her. *Oh, Zann. Our little girl is growing up.*

The loneliness became unbearable around sunset, when Dabney realized she wouldn't be listening to Alex's prayers and tucking her in bed, the way she'd done every night for ten years. She poured a cup of coffee and took it outside to drink in the garden. Her thoughts went back to the earlier part of the day. Eliza, or Lizzie as Kiah called her, wasn't at all how Dabney had pictured her. She knew she'd be beautiful to have won Kiah's heart. But Lizzie's reaction to Alexandra's blunder was surprising. The woman was unduly kind and went to extremes to comfort the child. Anyone who was good to Alexandra could win Dabney's heart in a minute.

Dabney was outside when she heard a strange noise coming from the big house. Like a scream. Then another and another. She ran to the house and didn't bother to knock when she realized it was Mrs. Weinberger yelling, "Help me, please, somebody help."

Dabney ran up the stairs and found Lula standing over her son's body, lying on the bathroom floor. She bent down to check his pulse. "Have you called the doctor?"

Lula nodded. "An ambulance is on the way." She knelt down with her head lying on her comatose son's chest. "Wake up, darling. Wake up and speak to mother."

Dabney fought back tears. Now was no time to break down, but her mind kept taking her back to the night she found Mack in the exact same position and he never woke up. *Oh, Oliver, please don't die. Please.*

The terrifying sound of a siren pierced the air as the speeding ambulance raced up to the mansion. Within minutes the driver and his assistant had Oliver on a stretcher and with Lula by her son's side, they were whisked off to the nearest hospital. Dabney was thankful Alexandra wasn't there to witness it. After seeing her grandfather die, Dabney could only imagine the traumatic effect Oliver's death would have on the child. *But he's not dead. He's not gonna die. Please, Lord. Don't let him die.*

Dabney wanted to follow the ambulance, but she wasn't sure Mrs. Weinberger would approve. Would she feel it was inappropriate for the housekeeper to show up at the hospital? She paced the floor of the cottage for over an hour, before grabbing her purse and running out the door.

She ambled slowly up to the registration desk and mumbled. "Could you tell me what room I can find Mr. Oliver Weinberger?"

The receptionist looked through a pile of papers, shuffled them again, then excused herself and walked off. What seemed like an eternity later, she came back and said, "Mr. Weinberger has not been assigned a room. He's in ICU, having his stomach pumped. His mother is in the waiting room down the hall if you'd care to wait with her."

"Thank you, I will."

Dabney walked in the room and saw the preacher kneeling beside Mrs. Weinberger's chair.

Lula looked up, and yelled, "Get her out of here. It's all her fault."

A nurse walking down the hall ran in when she heard the ruckus. "What's going on."

Lula shouted, "I want that woman out of here and don't let her back in. If my son dies, his blood will be on her hands."

The nurse motioned for Dabney, who was more than ready to exit, though she had no idea why Mrs. Weinberger would possibly think she could've been responsible. After all, she hadn't seen Oliver all day. From the hall, she heard Lula announce to the room full of people, "She cooks for us. She put a pork roast in the refrigerator yesterday, and Oliver ate most of it last night. I'm sure it wasn't done. Pork can be fatal when it's not thoroughly cooked."

Dabney's mouth flew open. "I did this to Oliver? I cooked it as long as I've always cooked a pork roast."

The nurse shook her head. "You did nothing. Mr. Weinberger's stomach is being pumped because he overdosed on aspirin."

"How do you know?" Dabney sobbed.

"The medic saw Mrs. Weinberger pick up an aspirin box from

the floor and tuck it in her pocket when the patient was lifted to the gurney. She was screaming for the doctor to pump his stomach, which indicated she knew exactly what had happened."

"Then what reason would she have to think it could've been the pork roast?"

The nurse's lip curled. "I've known Mrs. Weinberger most of my life. She wouldn't want anyone to think her darling Oliver had reason to want to end his life. That might somehow reflect on her. So she went after the closest scapegoat, which happened to be you."

"Under the circumstances, I should go. Would it be asking too much to have you call me if there's any change?"

"I'll be happy to. Leave your number at the nurse's station. What time do you go to bed?"

"Don't worry about the time. I want to hear of any change. Besides, I'll be up late packing my things. I have a feeling I'll be looking for a job tomorrow."

At six-thirty Monday morning, the phone rang.

"Miss Foxworthy, this is Louise, the nurse. I'm getting ready to go off my shift, but I wanted to let you know Mr. Weinberger is out of danger. He appears groggy but my guess is that he doesn't want to answer questions. I think he's terribly distraught that his plan didn't work. What do you suppose would cause a man of his means to want to end his life?" The question seemed hypothetical since she didn't pause for an answer. "I've seen aspirin overdoses before, when the outcome wasn't so good, but thankfully Mr.

106

Weinberger arrived at the hospital before too much aspirin could be absorbed in his system."

Dabney thanked her for calling, then spent the next half-hour praising God for sparing Oliver's life.

Chapter Fourteen

Three o'clock Monday afternoon, Dabney stood at the curb waiting for the bus.

Alexandra looked around and frowned. "Where's Oliver?"

"Let's go to the cottage and I'll try to explain."

Alex stepped inside and eyed the boxes stacked in the living room. "What's going on, Dabs?"

"Have a seat at the table while I get your milk and cookies."

"I want to know now. What's wrong? Why wasn't Oliver at the bus stop and why are you packing? We going somewhere?"

"Sweetheart, Oliver became ill and had to go to the hospital."

Alex's lip quivered. "He's not gonna die, is he?"

"No, no. In fact, he should be coming home very soon."

"What happened?"

"Seems he swallowed something he shouldn't have and it made him very sick."

"Something you cooked?"

"No, honey. It was nothing I cooked."

"Then why did you pack our things. I don't want to move."

"Neither do I, but—" She stopped to answer the phone.

"Yes, Mrs. Weinberger . . . yes ma'am. I'm sorry. No ma'am. Yes ma'am, I do understand. I'll be right over. I can have it ready before six. No problem."

She hung up the phone and grinned. "Alex, I need to run to the big house and throw something together for Mrs. Weinberger's dinner. Do you think you might could unpack boxes until I get back?"

"Yippee! I'm glad you changed your mind. I like it here."

Dabney had no idea what to expect. Would Mrs. Weinberger continue the accusations? Even if she did, Dabney would keep her mouth shut. This job was too important to both her and Alex to blow it. Not that she intended to work as a housekeeper for the rest of her life, but the pay was good, and she had hopes of going to business school at night as soon as Alex got a little older. She'd dreamed of being a secretary and dressing up every day in a pretty suit and heels like Ann Southern, in the picture show. With her organizational skills, she was convinced she'd make a great secretary.

For dinner, she made chicken and rice, a bean casserole, mixed green salad and a small peach cobbler. Mrs. Weinberger had two helpings of everything, though she complained that the chicken and rice was too salty, and the casserole too dry, which was a good sign. It meant things were back to normal, though normal in the Weinberger household was relative.

After dinner, Dabney puttered around the kitchen, taking longer than usual to clean up. Determined not to ask, she hoped Mrs. Weinberger would break down and mention Oliver's condition.

Seeing it wasn't going to happen, she hung up the apron, and was ready to walk out the door when Lula said, "Well, aren't you even going to ask about my son? If you're worried that I'm still angry because you almost killed him, I want you to know I've forgiven you. I'm sure you didn't intentionally undercook the meat. Just make sure it doesn't happen again. It could've been fatal, you know."

Dabney bit her lip and silently counted before speaking. "Thank you for being so generous. And how is Oliver?"

"The doctor says he can come home tomorrow. I have a little surprise planned for him."

"So, did you want me to cook something special for him?"

"Oh, it's a much bigger surprise than his favorite meal. My son and I will be going on a trip. I'm thinking New York City to take in a show and do a little shopping. Oliver needs a nice spring suit, and he could use a new pair of dress shoes. I'm thinking white. I'll never forget how cute he looked when he was six and had a pair of white Buster Brown's. He was such a handsome child. Come, let me show you the portrait I had made of him that year."

110

Although Dabney had seen the portrait every time she dusted the grand piano directly under the painting, she dutifully followed.

Mrs. Weinberger pointed and her eyes twinkled. "See what a darling he was in his cute little knickers, smocked shirt and white Buster Brown shoes?"

"Yes ma'am. I'm sure you were very proud of him."

"Well, naturally. I was the envy of every mother in Goat Hill. Oliver's a good boy. He's always been such a good boy. He was never like those other little hoodlums growing up in Goat Hill, sliding in the dirt playing ball, roaming through snake-infested woods and swimming in that dirty ol' creek every summer. Why, if a child had been drowning, there were so many kids at that old swimming hole, yelling and laughing to high heaven, no one would've noticed they were gone until it was too late."

"So, Oliver didn't go swimming?"

"Of course not. Weren't you listening?"

"Yes ma'am. Sorry. Mrs. Weinberger, if there's nothing else, I'll go check on Alexandra and cook her supper. She didn't eat before I left."

"You mean dinner."

"No ma'am. I mean supper. At my house, we have breakfast, dinner and supper." And with that, Dabney hurried out the door, before she opened her mouth one more time too many.

****

Tuesday morning, Dabney prepared fried chicken, fried okra, purple-hull peas and creamed corn. All Oliver's favorites. She watched out the window for Lula's Packard to pull up in the driveway.

Her heart hammered when he stepped out of the car. She wasn't sure why. Perhaps she was simply elated that his near-death experience was his own doings and not something she could've caused. Or perhaps she was looking forward to the compliments that were sure to come, after he finished the meal. Oliver was generous with his compliments, making it a joy to cook for him. Or maybe . . . just maybe, she was beginning to fall for this tall, gangly man with a heart of gold. She shuddered at the thought.

After lunch, Lula insisted Oliver go upstairs to rest, but he assured her the sunshine would do him good.

Lula said, "I'm sure you're right, dear. You do look pale and sitting in the garden would be good medicine. I wish I could keep you company, but if I don't show up for Bridge, the ladies will never forgive me."

"I wouldn't think of stopping you, Mother. Please don't worry about me. I'm fine. I would like for Dabney to accompany me though, if you could spare her. I could use the company."

"Well, of course you could, son. Suppose I call Sallie Belle to come keep you entertained. I'm sure she'd love to see you."

"No, Mother. How many times do I have to remind you I'm not and never will be interested in Sallie Belle Sellers."

Oliver persisted. "Mother, would you please ask Dabney if she'd do me the honors of keeping me company in the garden?"

Though Lula whispered, Dabney heard every word. "Oliver,

dear, do you really think it's advisable? I'd hate for the hired help to get the wrong idea."

"You have no need to worry, Mother. I'll make sure she understands my intentions."

"That's wise, son. See that you make yourself clear. I may be late getting home. It's warm outside now, but when the sun sets, it'll cool off. You'll need to wear a sweater."

"Yes, Mother."

Dabney pretended not to have overheard the conversation, when Oliver walked into the kitchen.

"Dabney, could you spare me a few minutes of your time?"

She dried her hands on a dish rag. "Sure. I've finished cleaning up. What can I do for you?"

Oliver crooked his arm, and escorted her out the door, into the Kipling section of the garden. "Shall we take a seat on the concrete bench?"

Dabney nodded. "This is my favorite garden. I could spend hours on end, sitting here. I feel like I'm in a beautiful jungle."

"That was the idea."

"What do you mean?"

"It's named for Rudyard Kipling, who wrote The Jungle Book. I named it that because of the exotic plants in this section."

"Alexandra has that book, but I didn't know who wrote it. Rudyard Kipling, you say? I'll have to remember that name. It sounds so romantic."

Oliver laughed.

"You're laughing at me. Did I say something wrong?"

"No, you said something right. My father's mother was related to the famous English poet. Her name was Anna Grace Kipling. I was named after her."

Dabney frowned, almost afraid to ask the next question. "Your mother named you Anna Grace?"

When he ceased from laughing, he said, "No, but she probably would have if my father had gone along with her. I think I was a big disappointment to my mother. She's told me many times how she cried when I was born, since she was sure she was having a girl. My full name is Oliver Kipling Weinberger."

Oliver seemed to enjoy being in her presence and for reasons she couldn't explain, she was beginning to look forward to moments they could be together.

Oliver had never met anyone like Dabney Foxworthy. She was beautiful, funny and very humble. She made his heart flutter and his palms sweaty. If this wasn't love, he couldn't imagine what it could be. But why kid himself. A beautiful, intelligent woman like Dabney would never be interested in someone like him. He was a joke. Always had been.

"What's wrong, Oliver?"

"Wrong? Why do you ask?"

"Your mood changed. I thought we were having a grand time, and then you seemed to withdraw. What's on your mind?"

"If I told you, you'd probably go pack your bags, leave and

114

never look back."

"You're teasing, now."

His brows meshed together. "Dabney, I know the day's coming when you'll want to leave. I'm dreading that day, already. I've never had a friend like you. My friends have always been the kind my Mother could buy for me."

"Oliver, I think you're wrong. You shouldn't sell yourself short."

"Dabney, I know what people say about me. I'm sure you've heard. People believe what they want to believe and nothing I can do or say will sway their opinion. So, why waste time wanting the impossible?"

Her eyes squinted into tiny slits. "Exactly what is it you want, Oliver?"

"I want to be able to walk down the street and feel like a man."

"That's silly. You *are* a man."

"I mean the kind of man a woman could feel proud to have as her escort. Forget it, I can see you don't have a clue what I'm trying to say."

"Yes, I do, Oliver, and I understand."

"Do you?"

"I do." She smiled. "You want a manly make-over."

He smiled. "I guess you do understand. Hopeless, right?"

"Not at all. I see a lot of potential hiding behind a door that you've been afraid to open. Would you like me to help you create that new image?"

"Dabney, you're sweet. But can't you see? I'll never be able to change people's perception of me."

"Tell me, Oliver. What do you see when you look in the mirror?"

"The same thing everyone else sees. A pale, gangly, four-eyed milksop, sporting clothes and a hairstyle left over from my father's era. Little Lord Fauntleroy, six-feet tall." His gaze stayed fixed on the ground. "Pretty embarrassing to admit, but it's true. That describes me perfectly, doesn't it?"

"Oliver, we're going to have a do-over and it's gonna be such fun. When you look in the mirror, I want you to see what I see—the strong, compassionate, handsome man that lurks beneath the surface. He's inside you, Oliver. We just have to figure out how to bring him out. But I think it's time for the bus. Would you mind meeting Alexandra? She'll be so happy to see you up and about. I need to get in the kitchen and start dinner, before your mother returns and finds me lollygagging."

Chapter Fifteen

Dabney could hardly wait for Thursday afternoon, when she'd have the whole afternoon to spend with Oliver. Funny, how he'd described what he saw when he looked in the mirror, and she couldn't deny it was exactly the way she saw him the first time they met. Not anymore. Now, she saw the real man that lay dormant underneath the uncomely façade. It was time for Oliver to see what she could see.

He met her in the garden at two-o'clock. "Dabney, I laid awake all night, thinking about what you said. I appreciate your wanting to help, but I'm afraid it's hopeless. Besides, if Mother catches on that you're participating with changing my persona, she'll fire you. I don't want you to leave."

"Then, she won't know. We won't make a drastic change, all at once. The idea is to change one little thing at the time and let your Mother and others get accustomed to seeing it. Sometimes, it might be such a little thing, they won't even notice. Then, we'll gradually add another change and then another. In six months, they won't even realize when it happened."

"Sounds too good to be true. What would you say is the first thing I should do?"

"Something small. Remember, this has to sneak up on your mother, bit by bit." She cocked her head and stared. "Hmmm . . . "

His face turned red. "It makes me nervous for you to look at me."

She laughed. "Why should it make you nervous?"

"Because what you're looking at is not what I want you to see."

"Oh, Oliver, if you only knew what I see when I look at you." Now, she was confident *her* face was red.

He reached for her hand. "Dabney, I've prayed for someone like you to come into my life for a very long time."

She managed to pull away. "Hey, don't get sentimental on me. We have work to do, mister." She ran her fingers through his hair, changing the mid-part to a part on the left side. "Nice."

"You think the hair should be my first change?"

"No way. A side part is a very good look for you, but it's almost too good."

Oliver laughed. "If I could believe that, I'd never part it in the middle again."

"Oh, it's true, but definitely too noticeable to begin the makeover. As I said, we need to go slow." She ran her hand down the buttons on his shirt. "Oliver, the ruffled shirts have to go.

Where do you even find them in this day and age?"

"Mother orders a half-dozen every fall from New York."

"Well, on your next trip to Dothan, go by Blumburgs and buy three or four plain white shirts and a pair of navy blue Oxford baggies."

He flinched. "Ooh, Mother hates the new baggy pants. I can hear her now."

Dabney dropped her gaze. She didn't want to see his expression. "Oliver, I mean no disrespect to your Mother, but you're listening to the wrong voice. Tune her out. Listen to your own inner voice." She expected him to bolt and defend Lula. But he didn't. One step in the right direction.

"Dabney, would you go with me and help me shop?"

"I couldn't possibly go, even if you needed me. And you don't. Alexandra will be getting off the bus in an hour, and besides, you need to learn to buy your own clothes."

"I know, and I want to. But I'd like to have you there to make sure I know what I'm doing the first time. Please? We'll make it a fun outing. Afterward, I'll take you and Alexandra to Zeke's for a steak dinner."

"I'll go with you shopping but not to that fancy restaurant. Let's go to F. W. Woolworth's for a hot dog and a milk shake for supper. Their hot dogs are delicious."

He chuckled. "Oh, yeah, not dinner. It's supper. I forgot. Sounds like fun. I've never had a hot dog."

"You're kidding! Then you're in for a treat, my friend."

"I'm not sure what I should tell Mother. She'll want to know why I'm not having dinner with her."

"Step number one, Oliver. If you want others to see you as a man, you have to first see yourself as one. Not as a little boy, tied to your mother's apron strings. You tell her the truth. Tell her you're going to Dothan to buy a few things and not to wait up."

The corner of his lip curled upward. "Dabney, you make it sound so simple. Mother will never let it stop there. She'll insist on going with me."

"Then, you thank her, but let her know you have a friend who'll be accompanying you."

"She'll ask who."

"Oh, Oliver, Oliver! You don't owe your mother an explanation for your every move. Begin now, by teaching her how to turn loose of her baby boy. If you can't, then all the changes in the world in your appearance won't change people's perception of you." This was going to be even more difficult than she'd imagined.

****

Kiah walked in from work, all smiles, with a large box under his arm.

Lizzie eyed the package and grinned. "Honey, I know I've acted silly, lately, giving you a hard time for no reason at all. Forgive me?"

He laid the package on a chair and kissed his wife. "No apology necessary, although I'll admit I've racked my brain trying

120

to figure out what I've done to upset you." He sniffed. "Dinner ready?"

"Uh . . . yes, but the package?" She giggled. "Did you forget?"

"Oh, I did. Look and see what you think." He handed her the box. "It's just a little something I bought for Alex. I passed by Morgan's Five & Ten show window this morning on my way to the bank, and it caught my eye." He reached in the bag and pulled out a beautiful bride doll, with jet black curls and a bridal ensemble complete with long, flowing train and a veil attached to a pearl-studded crown. "I think she'll love it, don't you?"

Lizzie hadn't seen Kiah this excited over anything in a long time. "It's beautiful, but what possessed you to buy her a doll?"

"I don't know. An impulse, I guess, but I'm glad I acted upon it. It was the only one in the store. I can't wait to give it to her. Why don't you call Dabney tomorrow and invite them to come over for dinner one night next week?"

Kiah patted the doll's curls, fluffed the dress, lifted the hem and admired the tiny white satin shoes.

Lizzie picked up the sack and the receipt fell out. "Kiah Grave. Please tell me you didn't really spend sixty-five dollars on a toy."

He grinned. "Outrageous, huh? Couldn't resist. I'd already made up my mind she had to have it before I walked in the store. I'm a sucker, I know."

"Not only outrageous. It's stupid to throw away money frivolously."

"Hey, no need to get nasty. It's not as if we don't have the money."

"Well I don't like the idea of giving such expensive gifts to a child we hardly know and I'm taking it back, tomorrow. She may not play with dolls and might even find it offensive. She's at least eleven, maybe twelve."

"She was ten, the twelfth of August."

So he knows her birth date? Lizzie ran to the bathroom and threw up.

Chapter Sixteen

Alexandra was working on her homework in the cottage when the phone rang.

"Alex, this is Mrs. Grave."

"Hey, Mrs. Grave. Dabney isn't here. She's over at Mrs. Weinbergers, but you can't call her over there because Mrs. Weinberger will get mad."

"Oh, but I'm not calling Dabney. You're the one I want to talk to."

"Really? What did I do? Did I say something I wasn't supposed to?"

"No, dear."

"So you aren't mad at me about something?" Alex relaxed when she heard her laugh.

"Of course not. Why would I be mad?"

"Hmm . . . sometimes I talk too much and I don't even know what I've said. You scared me when you said you were calling to talk to me and not Dabney. I thought I messed up."

"You can relax. You were a sweetheart. I'm calling because I was sorry we didn't get a chance to have that ice cream I promised. Perhaps you'd like to come over this afternoon and share a big bowl with me. I have homemade chocolate."

"Jeepers, I love chocolate, but I can't. I'm not supposed to bother Dabs while she's working and I'd have to ask her if I could go."

"I wouldn't want you to bother her, but I'm sure she wouldn't mind if you were with me. What if I have you back home before she gets off, so she won't worry? What d'ya say?"

"I guess she wouldn't mind, since you're married to Kiah Grave."

"Exactly. Dabney likes Kiah a lot, doesn't she? I mean, they were really good friends at one time."

"Yes ma'am. Really, really good friends. But I can't say anything else or I'll get in big trouble. I promised Dabs."

"I see. Well, sweetheart, I wouldn't want to get you into trouble, so maybe we should forget about having ice cream and we'll forget that I called you. I won't tell if you won't. That way, we'll make sure no one misunderstands. Good bye, Alexandra."

Dabney walked in and closed the screen door behind her. "Who were you talking to?"

Alex's eyes widened. "What are you doing back so early?"

"I came to get my bottle of cinnamon. Mrs. Weinberger is out, and I've already cut up the apples for a cobbler. Now, who was that on the phone?"

"Oh, Dabs. Do I have to tell?"

Dabney's pulse raced. "What's going on Alex?"

"Okay, but don't let her know I told you."

"Let who know what, honey?"

"Mrs. Grave."

"Mrs. Grave? She called you? Why? What did she say?"

"She wanted to come get me so we could eat ice cream at her house, but then she changed her mind."

"I don't understand."

Alex lifted her shoulders in a shrug. "Neither do I."

"Did she tell you not to tell me?"

"I think so."

"Alex, either she did or she didn't. Tell me exactly what she said."

"You don't like her, do you?"

Dabney rolled her eyes. "I didn't say that."

"You didn't have to. I can tell. But I don't think she likes you, either."

"What makes you say such a thing?"

"Because I know why she called. She didn't really want me to have ice cream at her house. She just wanted to know if you liked her husband and as soon as she found out that you do, then she was ready to hang up."

Dabney's jaw dropped. "Alexandra! You told her that I like

125

Kiah?"

"You do, don't you?"

"Yes, but not the way I'm sure she—"

When Alex began to cry, Dabney wrapped her arms around her. "Oh, sweetheart, I'm sorry, I didn't mean to scold you. You did nothing wrong, but I'm afraid Mrs. Grave may have misunderstood."

****

Tuesday evening, Kiah came home from work, walked in the parlor and leaned over his wife's chair to give her a kiss.

Lizzie turned away, then continued to read the book in her lap, without acknowledging his presence.

"Something coming from the kitchen smells good. I hope it's what I think it is. Did Cleo make liver hash?"

"Yes. But I'm not very hungry. Why don't you eat without me tonight?"

"You sick?"

"No. I told you I'm not hungry."

"What's wrong, Lizzie?"

"Nothing."

"Then why the cold shoulder?"

"Please, Kiah, just leave me alone."

"Lizzie, this is not like you. Something's going on and I want to know what it is."

"Go eat your dinner, Kiah. I'm in no mood to talk."

Lizzie went to the bedroom early and closed the door. Kiah learned long ago when she went through one of these hormonal moods of hers, it was best to leave her alone and wait for it to pass. For eight years she'd tried to get pregnant. If only he could convince her that she was all he needed. Sure, a kid would be great, but he'd never felt his life was empty with Lizzie. Why couldn't she believe him?

But when he saw she'd laid his pajamas, a pillow and a quilt on the sofa, he knew this was not the normal monthly mood swing. She'd never kicked him out of the bedroom before.

He opened the door to their bedroom, and sensed she was awake, though she pretended to be asleep. He sat down on the edge of the bed. "Honey, don't do this to me. I can't stand it. I've got to know what's going on with you. What have I done?"

Tears seeped from the corners of her clenched eyes. He leaned over and kissed her on the forehead. "Tell me, baby. Let me fix it."

She opened her bloodshot eyes. "Some things can't be fixed, Kiah. Did you send for her? Is that why she's here?"

His back stiffened. "Lizzie, honey, I have no idea what you're talking about. Did I send for who?"

"You know who."

He rubbed his hand over his forehead and tried to think. "Are you talking about Dabney? Is that what this is all about?"

"Yes. You were in love with her once, weren't you? Maybe you still are."

"No, Lizzie. I was never in love with Dabney. We were close

127

friends, yes. She lived next door to me when I was in high school, and well, we were sort of thrown together, but in love with her? No way."

"But you had a child together."

Her words took his breath away. "No, no. It's not true. You've been talking to Alexandra, haven't you? She told you about the birth certificate, but I can explain."

"Birth certificate?" She glared, then said, "No explanation necessary, Kiah. I think I've heard enough. Now, if you'll kindly leave the room, I want to go to sleep."

"Oh, Lizzie, you have it all wrong." It was obvious she wasn't going to listen to anything more he had to say. Not tonight. Maybe never.

Chapter Seventeen

Friday morning Lula Weinberger sat at the dining table, grumbling as Dabney poured her coffee. "What has gotten into that boy? He knows I'm a stickler for having breakfast on time. What could be keeping him?"

Oliver rushed in, leaned over and pecked his mother on the forehead. "Sorry, I'm late."

"The omelet is getting cold. What took you so—" Her jaw dropped. "Oh, my lands, please tell me those baggy pants are a joke. You aren't seriously considering wearing them in public, I hope."

He took a seat and picked up the omelet platter. "Sorry, you don't approve, Mother, but I rather like them."

She chuckled. "Dear, you can't be serious. You look like a common laborer. I can abide by the shirt for casual wear, but not for the office. The ruffle shirts I buy for you set you apart as the successful attorney that you are."

"Mother, could I pour you some orange juice?"

"Oliver Weinberger, don't change the subject. I demand you go upstairs and take off that hideous outfit after breakfast. You do remember that I have the Ladies Conference in Eufaula this weekend, don't you? I'll be leaving mid-morning but should be back Sunday afternoon."

He hid his smile with his fist. "I'd forgotten about the conference."

"Should I cancel?"

"I wouldn't hear of it."

"Well, dear, I do hate to leave you all alone in this big house, but Dabney is an excellent cook, so I'm sure she'll take good care of you while I'm gone. Now, tell me where you found the hideous garb you're wearing and I'll take it back first thing Monday morning."

Oliver glanced toward the kitchen and saw Dabney watching for his reaction. One look was all it took to strengthen his resolve. "Thank you, Mother, but that won't be necessary. I hope you can grow accustomed to the new look, because I happen to like it. Now, if you'll excuse me, I have a lot of work waiting for me in the office."

"Sit back down, Oliver. I'm not through with you, yet."

"I love you, Mother, but there are gonna be some changes made, beginning with oxford baggies and ruffle-free shirts." He grabbed another biscuit off the platter and stuffed in his mouth as he turned to leave. "Have a good day."

How one pair of pants and a shirt could make such a difference in one's mood was a mystery to Oliver, but he'd never experienced such an exhilarating feeling of freedom. He could hardly wait for Dabney to complete the project. She was right to take it slow. If a pair of baggy pants could cause such a reaction, a complete make-over could've caused his mother to have a coronary.

Oliver watched the clock all morning, eager for lunch. When Dabney served his plate, he reached up and grasped her by the hand. "How long will it take for you to pack this lunch in a picnic basket?"

"Ten minutes, top."

"Swell. Throw in a table cloth. We're gonna have a picnic down by the bay."

After finishing off the fried chicken, scraping the potato salad bowl for the last bite and devouring four fried apple tarts, Oliver stretched out on the grass under a large live oak tree and watched as Dabney took off her shoes and waded into the water.

"Dabney, why are you doing this?"

"It feels good to my feet. Little minnows are nibbling at my toes. It tickles. Pull off your shoes and come wade with me."

"I'm not asking why you're wading, Dabney. I'm asking why you're being so nice to me. No girl has ever taken an interest . . . unless of course, she was after the family fortune."

Dabney stomped out of the water and grabbed her shoes.

"What's wrong?"

"Is that what you think, Oliver? That I like you because you're rich?"

"No, you misunderstood. That's not what I meant at all. Please, sit down. I'm not ready to go. I've cancelled my afternoon appointment, so we don't have to be back until time for the bus." Dabney sat back down on the grass and her last sentence danced in his head. *She did say it. She said, you think I like you because you're rich? She likes me?* He laughed out loud.

"What's funny?"

"Just thinking of Mother's reaction." He knew Dabney assumed he was referring to Lula's reaction to the new and improved Oliver, but his mind had gone beyond the make-over. For the first time in his life, Oliver had something he really wanted that he'd have to get for himself, because what he wanted was something his mother couldn't buy.

"Oliver, you handled Step One with finesse this morning. Ready for Step Two?"

"I'm ready for the whole works, Dabney. What comes next? The hair?"

"No, we're not there, yet." She cocked her head and studied his face. "Didn't you tell me you see as well without your glasses as you do with them?"

"Actually, I think I see better without them, since the plain glass sometimes causes a glare. Mother purchased my first pair of non-prescription glasses the year I left for college, saying the

132

professors would pay closer attention to me if I appeared studious."

Dabney reached up and lifted them from his face. "Ah . . . I like it. But the glasses are Step Three."

"So what's the second step?"

"A new suit."

His brow furrowed. "But I have a closet full of suits. Mother has them tailored to fit me."

"No more fitted suits. I've been looking in the Sears & Roebuck catalog and all the modern men are not only sporting baggie pants, but the suit jackets are big with padded shoulders. What do you think?"

"Swell! Let's do it. I'd like to look thicker through the shoulders. It'd make me look heavier, and I could use a little extra weight. So will you and Alexandra go on another shopping spree with me tomorrow?"

"Not this time. You need to do this on your own."

"But what if I choose the wrong thing?"

"You won't. I have a feeling you know what you like, you've just been afraid to express yourself. Try on several and get the one that makes you feel good when you see your reflection in the mirror. That'll be the right suit for you."

Sunday morning, Oliver drove Dabney and Alexandra to church. Dabney tried to ignore the glares, when he escorted them toward the front. She could imagine the thoughts going through the busy minds, as they all wondered if Lula's boy would be brazen enough to sit with the housekeeper when his mother returned.

After services, four people commented favorably on Oliver's new suit, which appeared to please him. He slipped off his glasses and tucked them into his coat pocket. The way he threw his shoulders back and lifted his head, it was plain to see he was beginning to see himself in a different light. Dabney looked at the glow on his face, and her heart fluttered. He did look different. Had Oliver changed so drastically? Or had she?

Maybe it wasn't too soon to take the next step.

Monday morning, Dabney walked into the dining room with a tray of biscuits. Mrs. Weinberger huffed and drummed her fingers on the table as she waited for Oliver's entrance.

Dabney could hear him whistling as he bounded down the stairs. He strolled through the door, wearing a big smile, baggy pants, a plain white shirt, a snazzy argyle vest—and no glasses. Dabney knew he'd purposely not mentioned the vest, wanting to surprise her, and surprise her, he did. He glanced her way and she gave a quick wink of approval.

His mother frowned and Dabney could only hope she hadn't witnessed the wink.

Lula placed her napkin in her lap. "That will be all, Dabney. While we eat breakfast, I'd like for you to go upstairs, gather the dirty laundry and drop it down the shoot."

"Yes ma'am, but did you forget I did laundry yesterday?"

"Do as I say, please. You'll find a few pieces that I removed after you washed. You can wash them out by hand."

"Yes ma'am." Why did she have the peculiar feeling that Mrs. Weinberger was more interested in getting her out of the room than she was in having a few items washed?

Lula pounded her fist on the table. "Oliver Weinberger, what on this green earth has happened to you? Have you lost your senses? You look like one of those thugs that hang out in front of the pool hall with that ridiculous garb you're wearing. And where are your spectacles? As soon as you finish breakfast, go upstairs and dress like the gentleman I raised you to be. This is not Halloween."

"Sorry, Mother. You may as well get accustomed to the look. I happen to like it. Pass the biscuits, please."

Lula thrust her hand over her heart. "I'll find out what's behind all this tom-foolery and end it here and now. You're acting like a child."

"No, Mother, for the first time in my life, I'm acting like a man."

"It's that maid, isn't it? Don't think I haven't noticed the way you ogle her when she walks in the room." Her eyes darkened. "Oh, m'goodness, I see it written all over your face. It's her. It *is* her. She's the one encouraging you to dress like a . . . a commoner. I suppose that's all she's accustomed to being around. Really, Oliver, are you going to allow a cook to dictate how you should dress?"

"Mother, I've dressed the way you've dictated all my life. Now, it's time for me to make a few of my own decisions, and I happen to like baggy pants and plain-front shirts, so get used to the new me."

Lula rolled her eyes. "The new you, my foot! We'll see about that. I'll have to admit, she's a good cook and I'd hate to lose her, but I'll fire her in a heartbeat if you continue to allow her to put these foolish notions in your head."

Chapter Eighteen

Kiah returned home from work Monday evening to find Lizzie still in her gown and negligee. From all appearances, she'd not left the bedroom all day.

He lay on the bed beside her, but she turned her face to the wall. "Lizzie, honey, we have to talk. It's not the way you think. Alexandra is not my child. Have I ever lied to you before?"

His question caused her to slowly turn and face him. "I don't know, Kiah. Have you?"

"No! Never. Maybe I haven't told you everything about my past, but I think it's time. I don't want to keep anything from you." He pushed a lock of hair away from her eyes. "Lizzie, I've only loved two women in my life."

Her bottom lip quivered. "Me and Dabney."

"No. How many times do I have to say it? I've never been in love with Dabney. There was a time in my life when I wished I could love her, but I knew it wouldn't be fair to either of us to pretend."

"Then who was the other woman?"

"Actually, she was still a girl. Only seventeen when we first fell in love. Her name was Zann Pruitt, and she was Alexandra's mother."

Tears flowed from her eyes. "I knew it. You're Alexandra's father."

He locked his hands on top of his head. "Lizzie, aren't you hearing a word I'm saying? I'm *not* her father. Impossible. I had no idea Zann was pregnant." He jumped up. "Wait, I can prove it." He ran to the bureau and pulled out his leather attaché case. He unzipped a pocket and took out a yellowed letter and handed it to his wife. "Read it. I think you'll find it self-explanatory and it will prove I'm telling you the truth. This is a letter Zann asked Dabney to give me in the event of her death. No one has ever read it, but me. Not even Dabney. But I want you to know the whole story."

Lizzie gazed through clouded eyes at the signature at the bottom of the second page. How dare he be so brazen as to pull out love letters from a woman who gave him something out of wedlock that she hadn't been able to give him in all their years of marriage. He knew how her heart ached for a baby. She shoved the letter back. "Kiah, I can't read this. Why would you want to torment me this way?"

"I don't want to hurt you, Lizzie, but vain imaginations will hurt you far worse than the truth. You can read it yourself, or I'll read it to you, but you have to know the truth."

She wiped her eyes and silently read:

My dear, sweet Kiah,

If you're reading this letter, it means I've gone to be with the Lord.

Kiah, I've deceived the one person who means more to me than anyone else in this world—you. Not by choice, but I wasn't allowed to make my own decisions. Regardless of the shameful way my baby was conceived that dreadful afternoon, she's still my flesh and blood and I fought Mama and Daddy for the right to keep her. Now, it looks as if I'll lose her, anyway.

People in Pivan Falls will believe the baby's birth mother is Dabney, and that Mother and Daddy adopted the maid's baby. The idea was Dabney's. She's a real friend.

Kiah, I believe had I lived, you would've accepted little Alexandra with open arms and loved her as I do. It would be a lot to ask of most men, but you aren't just any man. You're very special. I have a couple of requests, and I have no doubt that you'll carry out my wishes if the time should come.

Mama insists my little Alex should grow up believing she's their adopted daughter and I'm her big sister. Maybe it's selfish of me, but to think she may never know I'm her mother, tears me apart. Tell her, Kiah. Tell her I said she's worth the price I paid for her. Tell her I loved her more than life. I've named my parents as Alexandra's guardians, but in the event of their death before she comes of age, I'm naming you as her legal guardian. I couldn't

139

fathom a better father for my little girl. I only wish you were.

I hate to leave you and Alexandra, but I'm confident God will send someone your way who'll love you as I do. She won't look like me, talk like me or act like me, so don't try to compare the two of us. Your love will be different, but just as strong as the love we shared.

When I was a little girl, I collected seashells. One morning I sat on the beach building sand castles when the tide rushed in and deposited a starfish at my feet. It was the most beautiful shell I'd ever seen. I left it on the sand, thinking it would still be there after I finished my castle. Minutes later, I looked up and the starfish disappeared when the tide ebbed.

Brokenhearted, I cried, but Daddy said, "You waited too late to retrieve it. Be patient, Zann, for God has many shells beyond the breakers, which will wash ashore with the incoming tide. The next one may not look like the one you lost, but will be equally beautiful. When it comes ashore, grab it, or it too, will disappear with the ebb tide."

So I sat on the beach that evening, waiting and watching. I'd almost given up, when the tide rushed in, and there on the beach was the prettiest pink conch shell I'd ever seen. This time, I knew what to do. I snatched it up, put it in my bucket and carried it home.

The tide's beginning to ebb, my darling, and soon I'll be no more. Don't mourn for what you've lost. God has something else in store. Watch for the high tide.

140

Until we meet again, all my love,
Zann

P.S. Dabney has instructions to give you this letter, if I don't make it. Please thank her for being such a wonderful friend. Goodbye, my darling.

With tears wetting her cheeks, Lizzie folded the paper and placed it in her purse. "Oh, Kiah, can you ever forgive me? That's the saddest letter. Poor Zann. Alexandra is such a beautiful child and her mother never had a chance to know her."

"Then, you do believe me?"

"It was wicked of me to ever doubt you."

"Lizzie, I've wanted to tell you about Zann so many times, but I wasn't sure you'd understand. The day I got off the train in Goat Hill and saw you, I immediately thought of Zann's words, and I felt in my heart the tide was finally coming in . . . that a new and lovely shell, unlike the one I lost, yet breathtakingly beautiful was washing ashore."

"Kiah, you both were so very young. And I do believe you weren't privy to what was going on at the time, and though I can't deny still feeling a bit envious, I'm glad you let me read the letter. But Alexandra said something about a birth certificate. What's that all about?"

He dabbed sweat from his brow. "It seems Zann gave my name as the father because she didn't want her little girl to have the stigma of a birth certificate with the words, *Father Unknown.* She also used Dabney's name while at the Home for Unwed Mothers, because of the ruse being carried out, she needed Dabney's name to appear on the birth certificate."

Zann threw her arms around her husband. "Oh, this is wonderful, my darling. Thank you, thank you for sharing this with me! If only I had known sooner."

Kiah had hoped she'd understand, but her ecstatic reaction took him by surprise. So much so, it frightened him.

Chapter Nineteen

Dabney made a point to stroll in the garden every afternoon while Alexandra was doing her homework, but not once all week did Oliver show up. He barely spoke to her when she served the meals.

His compliments on the food were fewer and with less enthusiasm than before. He'd even pulled out the stuffy-looking tailored suits.

The thought crossed her mind that in thinking she was helping, she'd caused him undue stress. Why didn't she leave things as they were? What business was it of hers if people called him a milksop? Gluing long ears on a hound dog won't change it into a bunny rabbit.

Saturday evening he lumbered into the kitchen while Dabney was cleaning up.

"Dabney, we need to talk."

Why did she feel a sudden urge to start bawling? She clamped her lips together and simply nodded.

"Meet me in the Kipling garden around seven?" He then

turned and walked out the door.

Dabney sat at the table with Alex while she finished her supper.

"Dabs, what time did Nelda Sue's mother say she'd bring her over?"

"Six-thirty."

She poked out her lips in a pout. "I thought so. She's late."

"Only five minutes, Alexandra. Be patient, she'll be here."

"Thanks for letting her sleep over. Can I go ahead and put down a pallet?"

"I think you'll have plenty of time for that. You girls never go to sleep before midnight."

"Dabs, is it me or do you think Oliver's been acting peculiar?"

"Peculiar? How do you mean?"

"I don't know. He doesn't talk to me much anymore. He doesn't laugh, either. He's becoming a bore."

"Alex! That isn't like you. We don't call people names."

"Sorry." Her small shoulders lifted in a shrug. "But it's true," she mumbled, though audible enough for Dabney to hear.

As a man thinketh in his heart, so is he, the Bible says. Was it worse for Alex to voice what Dabney was thinking in her heart? But if he was such a bore, why did she long to be with him?

Nelda Sue's mother, Lettie, hung around and talked for thirty minutes after arriving. Dabney tried to glace at the clock from time to time without being conspicuous. What if he thought she wasn't

144

going to show up?

At ten after seven, she left the girls playing paper dolls on the floor and rushed out the door. Oliver was sitting on a bench in the twilight.

"Sorry, I'm late," she said.

"Oh? Late? Are you?"

So, he didn't care if she came or not. Why did her heart feel as if it had been crushed into a thousand pieces? She blinked away the moisture in her eyes.

For years, Dabney had convinced herself that she was madly in love with Kiah Grave. Now, she realized it was nothing more than a puppy-love fantasy, which she kept alive through the years by fanning the flame. What she felt for Oliver, she'd never experienced before. Could it be she'd fallen in love with the milksop? Impossible. Or was it?

"Dabney, I suppose you've noticed the suits."

She nodded and prayed she wouldn't start bawling if she opened her mouth to speak.

"Well, I wanted to explain."

"No explanation necessary, Oliver. I judged you for allowing your mother to control you, when in fact I was doing the same thing. I was wrong to try to change you."

"No! I've never felt controlled by you. In fact, it was the opposite. A freedom like I'd never experienced before. I could hardly wait for you to see the argyle vests, because I picked them

145

out on my own. I liked them so much, I bought four."

The lump in her throat seemed smaller. "You looked spiffy in the baggies and vests, but I see you've gone back to your tailored suits, and if that's what makes you feel good about yourself, then that's what you should wear. Don't dress for your mother or for me, but dress for the man who stares back at you in the mirror."

"You don't understand. I hate the suits, but I've been left with no choice. As much as I detest them, I'll go back to ruffled shirts if it means allowing you to remain here."

"Allow me to remain here? But I'm not fond of the ruffled shirts. You know that. So what are you saying?"

"Mother suspects you have something to do with the changes I've made and she's threatened to fire you. She's been watching my every move for the past week. Tonight is her bridge party, and that's why I waited to meet you here. Dabney, I couldn't stand it if I thought I'd never see you again."

Dabney's heart did a somersault. "Oh, Oliver, no one's ever said anything so sweet to me before?"

"Then you aren't angry with me?"

"Angry?" She laughed. "I'm thrilled to know you'd go to such lengths to keep me around. But you won't have to, because Alex and I are leaving."

Leaving? The skin around his eyes tightened. "But why, Dabney?"

"Because I'm not gonna be responsible for you having to follow your mother's dress code. When I'm gone, she'll have

146

nothing to hold over you and you can dress the way you choose. If you choose ruffle shirts and old man suits, so be it. But if you truly like the latest look in men's fashions, then it will be your decision. My presence has begun to cause you undue stress, and for that I'm so sorry. I'll begin right away packing my things and will search for another job."

"You'd do that for me? Leave a job, with no guarantee of finding another one anytime soon, just to make things easier for me?"

"Of course. I'm . . . I'm very fond of you, Oliver."

"I don't want you to go, Dabney. Besides, it won't be easy to find another job. There aren't many people in Goat Hill wealthy enough to hire housekeepers. And even if you found someone, there's Alex to think about."

"Oliver, I won't stay here and let you become a puppet in order for me to keep this job. God will provide. I'm trusting Him."

"Please, Dabney. Don't leave. I know I'll never see you again if you leave."

"Oliver, I can help you change your outward appearance and your name, but you're the only one who can untie the apron strings that have you bound to your mother. You'll know where to find me, and if you come looking, I'll be waiting."

His eyes widened. "Waiting? For me? You mean that?"

"Of course, I mean it."

"I have an idea. Be ready in the morning at ten-forty-five and I'll pick you and the girls up for church."

147

"What about your mother?"

"She has a car."

"Oliver, don't do it for me. If you aren't doing this for yourself, it will end in disaster. Are you sure you're ready?" Trying to read his thoughts, she said, "You look serious. What are you thinking?"

"I am serious. I have a tough decision to make."

"I can't let you—"

"Can't let me do what? Make my own decisions? But I must, and this is a tough call." His lip turned up in a wry smile. "I'm trying to decide if I should wear the navy and yellow argyle or the black and gray. I think I'll go with black and gray. I bought a bow-tie to go with that one."

She cackled out loud. "Wow! I think I'm beginning to see a re-packaged Oliver, and I like what I see."

"Dabney, I want everyone to see a new Oliver. In fact, I wish I could change everything about the old Oliver. Right down to my name."

"But you have a nice name Oliver Kipling Weinberger." She giggled. "Mr. Kip Weinberger, I think I might be falling in love."

She could see his blush, even in the moonlight. "I've embarrassed you. I'm sorry."

"No, please don't apologize. You must know I'm in love with you, Dabney, but I thought it too much to hope for, to expect you to fall for me. Did you mean it?"

She reached up and caressed his cheek with the back of her

hand. "I should go in. The girls may have the house turned upside down by now."

Never had he wanted anything as much as he wanted to pull her close and feel her lips touching his, but for now, he'd have to be content in knowing she *might* be falling in love. Why risk doing anything that could cause offense? "See you in the morning?"

"We'll be ready."

He offered his hand and helped her up

Chapter Twenty

Sunday morning, with his Bible in hand, Oliver darted into the parlor, and gave his mother a quick peck on the cheek. "You look spiffy, Mother. Pink becomes you."

"Oliver!" She shrieked. "I will not have you driving me to church in those outlandish clothes. Get upstairs and put on something suitable. And I thank you for the compliment, but you know I don't approve of slang terms. Please refrain from using that silly word in the future. The word lovely would've been much more appropriate. Now run to your room and change." She flicked her hand, urging him to hurry.

"You'll need to take your car, Mother. I have a date."

"Don't be ridiculous. Go, go, go. You know how I hate to be late."

"Then you might want to get started, Mother, dear. I'll see you in church."

Dabney only had three dresses suitable for church, yet she'd managed to try on all three several times, before deciding on the yellow one. Alexandra and Nelda Sue waited out front for Oliver.

"Dabs, he's here," Alexandra yelled. "Do we have to sit with you and Oliver or can we sit on the front pew?"

"Can you girls behave?"

"We promise."

"Just remember, I'll be watching."

The girls strolled down to the front, and Dabney expected Oliver to choose a pew near the back, but he took her arm in his and escorted her three seats behind the girls. Her heart hammered. "Oliver, maybe this wasn't a good idea. I don't want to cause a ruckus."

"A ruckus?"

"You know . . . a scene. What if your mother—" Before she could complete her sentence, she looked up to see Lula Weinberger standing at the end of the pew, waiting to be seated. Dabney bit her trembling lip.

Oliver slid over, but Lula trampled over his feet and wedged her fluffy body between her son and the housekeeper.

Lula raised her brow. "Dabney, I didn't mean to interrupt. What were you about to say about me?"

Oliver butted in. "Mother, Dabney and I are pleased that you chose to sit with us, but if you don't mind, I'd like to sit beside my fiancé."

Dabney's throat tightened. *Did he say . . . fiancé?*

Oliver stood and stepped over his mother's feet and squeezed in between the two women.

Lula fanned her face, then thrust her hand over her heart. "Oh, Oliver. My chest. The pain is unbearable. I'm afraid I'm having a heart attack. Take . . . take me to . . . the hospital. Hurry, son."

Dabney nodded. "Go, Oliver."

He tossed her his car keys. "I'll drive Mother's car. You and the girls can drive my car home."

According to the doctor, Lula's angina pains weren't critical, but it was needful that she be kept calm and free of stressful situations.

Guilt-ridden, Oliver agreed to stay at the hospital through the night, to appease his mother, who insisted she was dying.

Lula pleaded with him to pull his chair to the edge of her bed and hold her hand. "Oh, Oliver, my precious boy, I want you to understand that I don't blame you, darling for this painful, near-death experience. I blame that gold-digger housekeeper who came here with the intention of setting her hooks into you. This is all her fault."

"Mother, you're wrong to blame Dabney."

Lula pulled back her hand and covered her ears. "Don't, son. I can't stand to hear you defend that low-life. Don't you see what she's doing? She's driving a wedge between us, and I fear you're so naïve, she's blinding you."

Before he could respond, Lula thrust her hand over her heart and moaned. "Oliver, dear, in case I don't make it out of here to fire her myself, I want you to go to the house the first thing in the morning and give her two weeks' salary and a notice of termination. I won't rest easy until I know she's gone and out of our lives forever."

"Mother, you can't mean that."

"I've never meant anything more in my life. I don't want that woman in my house."

Oliver tried to muster a smile. "And I suppose you're gonna do the cooking and cleaning? I don't see it, and you know how difficult it is for you to keep help. I think you might need to reconsider."

"I will do no such thing. You do as I say. That woman has got to go."

Then I go too, Mother. But he couldn't say it yet, not with her in her condition.

Chapter Twenty-One

Oliver left the hospital Monday morning at five-thirty. He wanted to have plenty of time to spend with Dabney while she prepared his breakfast.

He'd offer to help her and Alexandra find a temporary place to stay. She'd balk at taking money from him at first, but he'd make a formal marriage proposal and convince her that as her future husband, he'd soon be taking care of her and Alex for good. He simply needed to find her a place to live for a few weeks, until his mother regained her health and he could leave home. Was he being naïve to think she'd say yes to marrying him? What if she laughed in his face?

The discussion went much better than he'd anticipated.

"Oliver, you say you want to marry me. But does that mean after we're married that you intend for me to live in the house with you and your mother, because if that's what you're saying—"

"That's not what I'm saying. I just need time to get Mother

adapted to the idea of me leaving her." The excitement rose in his voice. "Honey, I've always wanted to move to a town where no one knows me. My life-long dream has been to do pro-bono work for people who need help. I want to live modestly, not the lifestyle to which I've been accustomed. I've done some checking in the past, and there's a little town about twenty-five or thirty miles from here, called Goose Hollow. I think you'd like it. It seems like a nice little community."

"Is there a school there?"

"Yes. It's quite small, but I'm sure Alexandra will meet some wonderful new friends. I'll get you settled in a boarding house, and then in three or four weeks, we'll find us a little apartment and tie the knot. How does that sound?"

"Oh, Oliver, I love you. Are you sure this is what you want?"

"Very sure, my darling. And it's Kip. Remember? It'll be easier to make the move while Mother is still in the hospital. When Alex gets home from school, the three of us will ride to Goose Hollow, and I'll get the two of you settled. I know it's sudden, but under the circumstances—"

"No, I want to go. I'll get Alex enrolled in school, and we'll be eagerly waiting for the day we can all be together." She reached up and swept his parted hair over to the left. "Kip, I think it's time for a new hairstyle."

He nodded. "I think you're right." He pulled a comb from his hip pocket and handed to her. "Say it once more."

"What? That it's time for a new hairstyle?"

155

"No. Say you love me once more."

"I do love you. I'm not even sure when it happened. I only know I've never felt this way before."

His hands shook as he gently placed them on her shoulder and pulled her close. She threw her arms around him, and when their lips touched, the feeling was indescribable. Never in his wildest dreams could he have imagined a woman with so much beauty and brains could fall in love with someone like him.

The thought of being married to such a sweet, beautiful woman, helping her to raise a precious little girl and doing something he really wanted to do brought prickles to the back of his neck. Not everyone gets a second chance for a do-over in life. If this was a dream, Oliver prayed he'd never wake up.

There were no boarding houses in the small town of Goose Hollow, but Oliver rented a quaint little log cabin in the edge of town for Dabney and Alexandra. Nothing fancy, but it was much nicer than Rooster Run, where she grew up. The cottage previously belonged to a family by the name of O'Steen, but had been donated to the local church. According to Oliver, the elders had made some renovations, including adding an indoor bathroom, and rented it out for a paltry sum. The modest cottage had been empty for quite some time.

Alexandra had fallen asleep before they reached the cabin. Oliver lifted her from the backseat.

Dabney said, "Just lay her on the bed and I'll slip off her shoes and change her clothes later."

Oliver walked back into the front room and sat on the couch beside Dabney. "I had the strangest feeling when I pulled the cover over Alex."

"What do you mean?"

"Like she was mine and that we were a family. A real family." He put his arm over her shoulder. "Oh, Dabney, it's as if I'm dreaming. Are you and Alexandra really real?"

"Oliver, are you sure you aren't rushing into this? You don't even know me. Not really"

"I know all I need to know. I know I want you to be my wife and Alex to be our little girl. What more could any man wish for?"

"What if I were to tell you that my name was a dirty joke among the high school football team when I was seventeen? And what if I told you that not all the rumors were true, but some were. I learned it from my mother, who put food in my mouth by being the town slut."

He pulled her closer. "You must've gone through some terrible times to feel so hostile toward your mother."

"You can't even imagine, Oliver. I vowed I'd never wind up like her, but then she died."

"And I suppose you realized then, how much she really loved you."

"No. I only realized that if I wanted to eat, I had to learn the profession, and I did, though I hated every minute of it."

"What about your father?"

"What father? There was this one fellow I called Daddy. I remember Mama called him Demp, He was the only one who ever took up time with me. Oh, how I loved that man, but like all the no-account rascals after him, he took off one day and I never saw him again. I suppose he only pretended to love me, to get close to my mother." She stood and walked over to the door. "Now that you know my past, can you honestly say I'm the kind of virtuous woman you want to marry?"

She opened the door and waited for him to walk out, although he remained seated on the couch. "I know I should've told you before now, Oliver, but I never expected things to go this far. When I realized that I was falling in love with you, I couldn't bring myself to tell you the ugly truth. But just now, when you walked back in the room and said I was the kind of woman you wanted to marry, I knew I had no choice. I had to tell you. The truth would eventually come out and you'd hate me for deceiving you."

He stood and walked to the door. With his forefinger he lifted her chin. "I thought I loved you when we walked in here tonight. But I find I love you even more with every breath you take. There's nothing you can ever tell me, Dabney Foxworthy that can make me stop loving you."

She threw her arms around his neck. "Oh, Oliver, I don't know what I've done to deserve you. You've made me so very happy."

He chuckled. "It doesn't take much to make you happy. How many women would be content to live in a little shanty in the backwoods, where she knows no one? You're one-of-a-kind, sweetheart. I feel guilty leaving you and Alex here. Are you sure you're okay with this arrangement?"

"Oliver, the place is perfect, and we'll be fine, so stop worrying. There's nothing more I could want. Alex and I are together and you've taken care of all our needs."

He reached in his wallet and pulled out folded bills. "Please, Dabney, won't you take it? I'd feel so much better."

"No, Oliver. We've gone over this. I still have a little money and I plan to look for a job. I appreciate your generosity, but I never want to feel like a kept woman again."

"But it's not the same. I'm going to marry you."

She reached up and pecked him on the cheek. "Yes, and when you do, I'll gladly take your money. Good night, my love."

He held her tightly, then placed a kiss on her lips. "Goodnight, sweetheart. I'll be back in a couple of weeks, but I'll write every day."

Dabney watched him drive away and wondered how she could've been so lucky to land such a wonderful man. She could hardly believe she was about to have a family of her very own—a man who loved her with all of his heart and a little girl who adored her. What more could any woman ask?

The few people she met in her first few days in Goose Hollow, all proved to be friendly. She was especially fond of Alex's teacher, Mrs. Marcy Woodham. Marcy had invited her to church, but explained the elderly pastor, known as Brother Charlie, was having a difficult time trying to take care of his church duties, while tending to his sick wife, even though they lived next door to the church.

Dabney was familiar with the little church, since it was walking distance from the cabin. "Thank you for the invitation. Lord willing, Alexandra and I will see you Sunday. I'm sorry to hear about your preacher's troubles. What's wrong with his wife, if it's not rude of me to ask?"

"To the contrary. I appreciate your concern. Miz Bertie, as we all refer to her, suffered a stroke a few weeks ago and although there are women in the church who take food by from time to time, what Brother Charlie really needs is full-time help, bless his heart."

Dabney's pulse raced, as she listened to Marcy talk about her beloved pastor. The job would be perfect. She had plenty of experience taking care of folks.

After arriving back at the cabin, she decided to walk over to the parsonage and apply for the job.

A tall, angular old fellow with a slow gait was walking from the church to the parsonage when Dabney arrived. Though his face was marked with pain, he managed a huge smile and offered her a trembling hand.

"Well, I don't believe we've met?" He said. "My name's Charlie Yancey. Most folks just call me Brother Charlie. You new in Goose Hollow or just visiting?"

"New. I'm Dabney Foxworthy." She pointed down the road.

160

"I'm renting the little log cabin, less than a mile from here."

"Oh, you're talking about the O'Steen cabin. It's been empty for a year or so, I reckon. Well, Miss Foxworthy, welcome to our neck o'the woods. Is there something I can help you with, or were you just passing by?"

"Please. Call me Dabney." She wrung her hands. "I . . . uh, that is, I heard from one of your church members that you might could use some help taking care of your wife. I'd like to apply for the job if it isn't already filled."

"Bless your heart, child. No, it isn't filled. We have a great congregation and they've been after me to hire a full-time caregiver. I just haven't been able to bring myself to letting someone else care for my precious Bertie. I promised sixty-two years ago to be there for her in sickness and in health. It's a privilege—but it's also my duty." Giant tears welled in his eyes.

Dabney reached for his hand. "And what did she promise?"

His eyes squinted. "I beg your pardon?"

"What did Miss Bertie promise you?"

He pulled out a handkerchief and wiped his mouth. "Well, now, let me see." He smiled. "The same thing, I reckon."

"That's what I thought. I'm not here to take over your responsibilities. I'm here for Miss Bertie, to help *her* take care of you. She needs me to wash and iron your clothes, clean the house and cook your meals. You just continue to do your job, and let me help Miss Bertie take care of her duties."

He grinned. "Now, that you put it that way, why should I

prohibit you from helping my darling Bertie? But before you accept, let me warn you she can't pay much."

Dabney felt a sudden urge to give the old man a hug. "I don't require much."

Surely God's favor was upon her to once again put her in a position to take care of one of His anointed. What a divine privilege it had been to care for Mack and now to be of service to Brother Charlie, Dabney felt doubly blessed. Mrs. Bertie was a dear and no trouble at all. If only Oliver's mother could be so kind. Although it came easier to still refer to him as Oliver in her thoughts, Dabney made a concerted effort to call him Kip in his presence, since it seemed to give him confidence that he was burying "Oliver's" old life with all its unpleasant memories and giving "Kip," the life that he'd only dreamed possible.

Oliver picked up the phone to call Dabney. The operator said, "Good morning, Oliver. How's your mother? I heard about her falling and breaking her leg. What a shame."

"Maude, you have it all wrong. Mama didn't break her leg."

"Well, I heard . . ."

He tuned her out. His explanation would go unheeded. By mid-afternoon, the gossips would have picked another subject.

"Maude, I'd like to make a long distance call, please."

"What town?"

He paused. "Nevermind." He placed the receiver back on the cradle. If he really planned to start anew, he'd need to begin now.

Long distance calls costs money. The old persona—Oliver with all his wealthy clients, wouldn't have thought twice about making the call—but since the new Kip would be working pro-bono, he'd be much more frugal. He reached in his desk and pulled out a fountain pen and three sheets of stationary.

My darling Dabney,

I trust you're as excited as I, and that sweet little Alexandra is adjusting well in her new classroom. The days seem so long without you, dear. Mother is still in the hospital, although the doctor insists she's ready to go home. But you know Mother. No one tells her what to do. Sallie Belle comes and sits every day, and you should hear the two of them when they get together. Like two peas in a pod. Sallie Belle's head begins to bob up and down before mama can finish a sentence.

Sallie enthusiastically agreed to take over the responsibility of finding a new housekeeper/cook and Mother told her to "make sure she's homely, because homely girls made the best household servants." I had to bite my lips to keep from laughing out loud. I was quite sure Mother didn't trust me around another pretty girl, but what she doesn't know is that Betty Grable couldn't turn my head. I've found the only girl for me.

I have several clients whom I feel an obligation to, but as soon as these clear, we'll be in a position to set the date. I'm excited that I'll finally be able to work pro-bono, and be married to the most wonderful girl in the world. I can't say it's what I've always dreamed of, as it far exceeds anything I dared dream.

Well, dear, I have to be in court in a few minutes, so I'll close for now. Give Alexandra my love and I hope to see you girls in a couple of weeks. Mother should be out of the hospital and hopefully, Sallie will have hired a cook. I'm not sure my Mother knows how to boil water.

Yours truly,

Kip

Chapter Twenty-Two

Lizzie stuck her head in Oliver's office door. "Too busy to see an old friend?"

"Never too busy for you, Eliza."

Her eyes squinted as she eyed him from the top of his head to the soles of his feet. "You look different. What have you done?"

"You approve?"

"Absolutely. But I can't put my finger on what's changed." Her jaw dropped. "It's your hair. You used to part it in the center. Well, I like it. It makes you look less . . ."

Oliver smiled. "Like a milksop?"

"That wasn't what I was going to say."

"Wasn't it?"

"No. I was about to say less stuffy, but then I decided that sounded judgmental."

"Well, maybe we've both changed, Eliza. The girl I once knew wouldn't have thought twice about speaking her mind. She may have even used the words Armadillo Face."

She flinched. "Ooh, about that. I'm so sorry. That was cruel of me to—"

"Forget it, Eliza. It was rude of me to bring it up."

"Oliver, since Mama died, no one calls me Eliza any more. I much prefer Lizzie. Eliza makes me shudder, because it sounds as if I'm being reprimanded. Sounds silly, I know."

"Not silly at all. I understand perfectly. I prefer to be called Kip instead of Oliver. Makes me feel more confident."

She laughed out loud. "You're poking fun, aren't you? Kip isn't your name."

"You're right. It's my nickname, just as Lizzie is yours. My name is Oliver Kipling, but I prefer Kip."

"Well blow me down. How does Lula feel about that?" She popped her hand over her mouth. "Sorry, that was not nice. But I couldn't help remembering the day she admonished my daddy for calling me Lizzie, and saying she hated nicknames."

He grinned. "Oh, I'm sure I'll never convince Mother to call me anything but Oliver and the folks here in Goat Hill will never say nor see me as anything other than Fauntleroy, Lula Weinberger's coattail boy. But I hope in time to correct that image."

When it appeared Lizzie had not heard a word he said, he leaned back in his swivel desk chair. "Now—to what do I owe this visit?"

Lizzie sucked in a deep breath. "Oliver, I understand that your mother's housekeeper—Dabney Foxworthy and her ward, little Alexandra are no longer in your employ and have moved elsewhere. Would you happen to know where they moved?"

"Sure. Dabney will be pleased to know you asked about her. She told me Alexandra had taken quite a liking to you and Kiah. They're renting a little log cabin in Goose Hollow." He smiled. "It's quite primitive, but it seems to suit her. Dabney's about as down-to-earth as they come. Not superficial like so many women I've known in the past."

She glanced down. "Like me?"

"Honestly, Lizzie, I wasn't referring to you. Actually, I had Sallie Belle in mind. However, now that you bring it up—"

After they both had a good laugh, Oliver said, "If you're looking for Dabney because you were hoping to hire her, I'm afraid that'll be impossible, since she already has another job."

"I'm glad to hear it, but I have a housekeeper, so that's not why I'm interested in her whereabouts. Oliver, what I'm about to tell you may shock you. I don't suppose Dabney told you whose child Alexandra is."

"In fact, she did. Alex's mother died shortly after she was born, and she was being raised by her grandparents." He shook his head slowly. "But it seems her grandmother is in a hospital for the insane and the grandfather died suddenly. Since Dabney was Alexandra's nursemaid and had cared for the child since birth, naturally, she was given custody. She's very devoted to that little

167

girl. Couldn't be any more loving if she were her own." He grinned. "So you see? Dabney tells me everything. We've become quite close."

Lizzie blew out a sigh. "That's good. I was afraid I might have to go into a lengthy explanation. I'll admit, I was jealous of Dabney when she first arrived, but after Kiah told me the truth about everything, I realized he isn't and never has been in love with Dabney Foxworthy. He admitted she was in love with him and he even considered marrying her and bringing her with him when he left Pivan Falls and moved here—not because he loved her, but he couldn't stand to leave her crying. He's such a softy. I'm certainly glad he didn't give in to her tears. I can't imagine being married to any other man and since you've become sweet on Dabney, I'm sure you share my feelings. She's a swell girl, and I'm happy for you both, Oliver."

Oliver tried to absorb the words, but it was almost too much to take in. Surely, Lizzie had misunderstood. Dabney in love with Kiah? No! Lizzie was mistaken. Dabney said they were neighbors and she was quite fond of Kiah's mother—but she mentioned nothing about ever having been in love with Kiah. His pulse slowed after convincing himself that Kiah had simply told Lizzie that he and Dabney were once close friends, and Lizzie, being Lizzie, had chosen to embellish the story to suit her. He glanced at his watch. "I don't mean to rush you, but I have an appointment in fifteen minutes. Am I right to presume this is a social visit, or is there something I can do for you?"

"Yes, I'd like you to represent us."

"I don't understand. What's going on?"

Lizzie reached in her purse, pulled out a piece of paper and handed it to him. "I sent for this last week, and it came this morning. You'll need to pull out your spectacles."

Oliver shrugged. "I don't wear them anymore. I see fine. So what've we got here?" He unfolded the paper and stared in disbelief. His jaw tightened. "Dabney Foxworthy, mother? Kiah Grave, father." *Birth certificates don't lie. But Dabney said . . .* He sucked in a lungful of air. There had to be a logical explanation. "Lizzie, I'm curious how Dabney happened to come to Goat Hill." He thumped a pencil on the desk several times. "I don't know how to ask this, other than just blurt it out. Do you suppose Kiah might've sent for her?"

She shook her head. "Oh, no, it wasn't like that. Dabney came looking for him, but only because she felt compelled to keep a promise she made when Alex was born."

"I don't get it. And you're okay with that?"

When tears came to her eyes, Oliver wanted to suck the words back in. "I'm sorry, that was callous."

"It's okay." *These tears are bittersweet.* "Surely you know how hard we've tried to have a baby. I've had three miscarriages and the doctor doesn't give me much hope of ever carrying a child full term. Alexandra is such a darling little girl, and Kiah and I both are crazy about her. I'll admit I was jealous of Dabney, but

169

when I realized the truth, I knew she'd done a very unselfish thing to come here. I know how much she loves Alexandra, and it'll be hard for her to give up the child; yet, she came, not just for Kiah's sake, but for Alexandra's. Not many women would be so unselfish."

His fuse grew shorter and shorter. What a jerk he was to think a pretty girl like Dabney could ever fall for a rube like him. *I'm stupid, stupid, stupid. She thought if she could coax me into marrying her, she'd be near her lover boy.* "So what do you need me for?"

"Kiah and I want custody of Alex. I was hoping you'd represent us, but I'm getting the impression Dabney has become more than just your Mother's former housekeeper. Not that I think she'll fight us, since it's become obvious that giving up Alexandra to Kiah was her reason for coming here, but I realize it could become very emotional for her when it comes time to sign the papers. I can see where it might place you in a peculiar position—a conflict of interests, as you lawyers say." After a long uncomfortable silence, she stood to leave.

His jaw jutted forward. "Sit back down, Lizzie. I'll be happy to represent you." How could he have been such a sap: Dabney had obviously come to Goat Hill to be near the man who fathered her illegitimate child. She concocted an outlandish tale about Alexandra's mother dying and then added the crazy story about the grandparents. Oliver jumped up and paced back and forth in front of his desk, with his hands clasped behind him.

170

"Oliver, are you okay? You look pale."

"Haven't you heard? Oliver is a milksop and we milksops are always pale."

Her pulse raced. "Did I do something wrong? You act as if you're angry with me."

"No, not you, Lizzie. I'm here to help you. If you want custody of Alex, I'll see you get what you want."

Chapter Twenty-Three

Dabney ran to the mailbox every evening, hoping to get a letter from Kip. She'd written him every day as they promised, but when her box was still empty after two-and-a-half weeks, she felt his mother had gotten through to him, convincing him that the prestigious Weinberger name shouldn't be tarnished by mixing with the hired help.

Finally, a letter came, postmarked Mt. Meigs, Alabama. Strange. It was addressed to Dabney, had her new address, but she'd never heard of a place called Mt. Meigs and couldn't imagine who could be writing her. She tore into the envelope and unfolded a three-page, typed letter inside.

Kilby Prison
Thursday morning

My dearest Dabney,
I know this is going to come as a shock to you, but I had a surprise visit this morning from your fiancé. He's quite a man. He loves you very much to have gone to such lengths to find me.

Dabney, he told me the sad life you had growing up, and to know it was all my fault is almost more than I can bear. Kip insisted I write to let you know you have a father; however, I can't imagine why he'd want you to know, after hearing my story. But here it is: Your mother and I married young. She was seventeen. I was eighteen. I thought she was the most beautiful woman I'd ever seen, and everywhere we went, she drew stares, she was so lovely. But I was insanely jealous, though looking back, I realize Hannah never gave me cause. Never. She couldn't help that she was beautiful. We had a nice farm that I'd inherited. Life was good. I'll never forget the day I came in from milking and Hannah had a feast set out on the supper table. I asked what the occasion was, and that's when I learned we were going to have a baby. I was ecstatic. Me, a father. Then you were born, and you were everything I could've wanted in a little girl. We were inseparable, and I never tired of hearing you call me "Daddy."

You were barely three, and Christmas was coming. Hannah bought you a baby doll and I made a doll bed and a high chair. We'd sneak them out at night, just to look at them after we put you to bed. We could hardly wait for you to see them.

Then four days before Christmas, I came out of the field to get a tool from the barn to fix the tractor. When I opened the barn door, I heard giggling. I looked up and there in the loft was my Hannah and Dooley Ames, the mailman. I can't explain the

173

rage that swept over me, seeing them. My rifle was standing by the door. I grabbed it and fired, hitting Dooley in the shoulder, though I aimed for his heart. I was sentenced to life in prison for attempted murder. Hannah came to visit me in jail, but I refused to see her. I told her I wanted a divorce.

It wasn't until the trial, three months later, that I learned Dooley had delivered a crab net that Hannah had ordered for me for Christmas. She asked him if he'd mind helping her get it in the loft, to hide it from me. There wasn't and never had been anything between Hannah and Dooley. I never heard from her after I came to Kilby, but always believed she remarried and the two of you lived happily ever after, with me out of the picture.

Dabney, my heart broke into a million pieces when Kip told me the dark path that Hannah chose and the kind of life you were subjected to, all because of me. I want you to know your mother was a fine woman. She was a faithful wife. I can only imagine she must've been so angry with me for accusing her of something she hadn't done, that in her own mind, she was paying me back.

I won't ask you to forgive me, because I know it's too much to ask. But Kip thought you should know that you really do have a daddy and that he loves you more than life itself.

Your daddy,

Dempsey Foxworthy

Daddy? I have a daddy? All her life Dabney assumed Foxworthy was her mother's maiden name. Now, to find out that she really did have a father and she even carried his last name, left her with mixed feelings.

She wanted to hate him for what he'd done. Not only to her mother, but to her. Yet, hard as she tried, she couldn't hate him. He'd done a terrible thing, but he loved her. He really loved her. She knew it, not just because he told her so, but because she remembered him. There were times in her past she wondered if she'd made him up. But he was real and she held the proof in her hands. He was the man her mama called Demp. The man she remembered riding her on his shoulders, playing with her in the creek and telling her bedtime stories.

But why didn't Kip write to let her know he found him? Dabney didn't like the negative thoughts sifting through her mind. Kip had promised to write every day, yet she'd only received one letter. Could it be that after checking into her background and discovering her father was a convict, he had a change of heart? Well, of course. That was it. There was no other plausible explanation. *I'd be stupid to think a smart attorney like Oliver Kipling Weinberger would still want to marry me, after learning I'm the offspring of a prostitute and a jailbird.*

When she carried Mrs. Bertie her medicine, the gentle white-haired lady said, "Sugar, you've been moping around like a mother hen who can't find her biddies. Like to talk about it? I may not help much, but I've been told I'm a pretty good listener."

Not that she felt like sharing her heart, but the elderly lady seemed genuinely concerned and for Mrs. Bertie's sake more than her own, Dabney pulled a chair up to the edge of the bed. "I suppose I let my head outrace my heart." She feigned a smile. "That made no sense at all."

"Why, it made a whole lot of sense. You're saying your heart tells you that you're in love, but your logic tells you not to listen to your heart."

"You're very perceptive. I thought I was being vague."

"Sweetheart, why don't you fix us a pot of coffee and let's talk about it. Sometimes being able to say it out loud helps put everything into perspective."

When Dabney came back with the coffee, Mrs. Bertie patted the edge of the bed and said, "Sit down here beside me, so I can hold your hand while you get it all off your chest."

The front door opened and Alex came running inside.

Dabney jumped up, shocked that two hours had passed since she first sat down and began pouring her heart out to the sweetest, wisest woman she'd ever had the pleasure of meeting. She repeated the verse that Mrs. Bertie had prayed for her. *I can do all things through Christ who strengtheneth me.* Though she believed with all her heart that Kip loved her, the invisible chains that linked him to his mother could never be broken, and Dabney had made it clear that she could never live with the domineering woman. Her heart was breaking, but with God's help and Mrs. Bertie's wise counsel, she and Alex would get through this. They'd weathered fierce storms before and came out on the other side. She had to believe she'd weather this one also.

Dabney walked Alex into the kitchen. "Hungry, sweetheart?"

"Starving. Got any pound cake left?"

"Look in the pie safe. I think there's a slice or two in there. How was your day?"

She lifted her shoulders.

Dabney poured her a glass of milk and sat down at the table with her, while she ate her cake. "You didn't answer me."

"I forgot what you asked."

"I asked the same question I ask you every day when you get in from school. How was your day?"

Again, she shrugged. "Okay, I guess." Her lip quivered.

Dabney reached over and placed her hand on Alexandra's arm. "What's wrong, honey. Did something happen at school?"

"I don't wanna talk about it."

"Alex, this isn't like you. If it's about a low grade on a test, don't let it get you down. You're smart and you'll be able to pull it up."

She burst into tears. "I hate this school. I want to go back to Goat Hill to school."

"Oh, sweetheart, I know it isn't easy having to change schools, but in no time you'll have made new friends, and you'll feel differently."

"No. You don't understand. I knew you wouldn't." She pushed back from the table without finishing her cake. "I'm going

177

for a walk."

"Don't you want to go in and speak to Mrs. Bertie? She can make a bad day turn good just with her smile. I was feeling blue myself, earlier, and after spending some time with her, I now feel much better. Go in and say hello."

"Maybe when I get back."

"Would you like me to go with you?"

Alex shook her head.

"Sure, kid. I think we all need some alone-time. Just don't wander off so far that you can't make it back before dark."

****

Lizzie Grave grabbed her hat and was heading out the door, when Alexandra came walking up the marble steps.

"Alex! What are you doing here?"

She hung her head. "I ran away. I hate Goose Hollow and I'm never, ever going back there."

Lizzie's heart pounded. "But how did you get here?"

"I hitch-hiked."

"Hitch-hiked? Oh, honey, it's extremely dangerous for a little girl to get in the car with a stranger. Please, don't ever do anything like that again. All sorts of bad things could've happened to you."

"Bad things have already happened to me."

Lizzie's words caught in her throat. Did she dare ask? "Honey, suppose we go sit in the parlor and you tell me exactly why you ran away."

"I'm thirsty. May I have a glass of water?"

178

"Sure. How about a glass of lemonade?"

Alex nodded. "Swell."

"Are you hungry?"

Again, she nodded. "But I don't wanna put you out."

"Well, aren't you sweet? It's no trouble at all. I think we have a couple of left-over pork chops in the Frigidaire."

"Sounds good. Glad it's not fried chicken. The old fellow who picked me up made me ride in the back of his truck with a big pen full of squawking chickens. There was hardly enough room for me to sit." She bit her lip. "I reckon I didn't exactly tell him the truth about why I needed a ride, but I figured he'd take me back to Goose Hollow if I told him the truth."

Lizzie shuddered. What could've been so bad that the poor child would've risked her life to come seeking shelter? She tried to hide her shock and rang for the maid. "Cleo, would you bring our guest a glass of lemonade and a pork chop?"

Cleo's brow creased together. "Did I hear that young'un say she hitch-hiked here from Goose Hollow?"

Lizzie's chin shot up. "Cleo! You aren't to concern yourself with affairs that are none of yours. Now, please, do as I said. She's hungry."

Chapter Twenty-Four

Dabney walked back to the kitchen window and looked out. There was no sign of Alex. She should've been back over an hour ago. Terror shot through her body like a bolt of lightning as wild imaginations robbed her of her logic.

She never meets a stranger. What if some thug talks her into getting in the car with him? She can't pass by a creek without taking off her shoes and wading. What if a moccasin . . . she shuddered. *Alexandra, where are you?*

Dabney tried to hide her concern when she carried Mrs. Bertie's supper to her. Brother Charlie picked up his plate and carried it into his wife's room, so they could eat together. He said, "I haven't seen Alexandra all afternoon. Is she visiting friends?"

Dabney feigned a smile to keep from alarming the elderly couple. "No, she went for a walk."

He glanced toward the window. "Not far, I hope. The sun's going down fast."

She nodded. "Yes, it is."

"I don't wish to pry, dear, but from the stressed look on your face, I gather you feel she should've been back before now. I'm sure she's fine. Probably stopped to visit a little friend and they're having so much fun, she hasn't realized how dark it's getting."

Dabney blew out a long breath. "I only wish that's where she was. I'm afraid that's a big part of the problem. She has no friends here and poor kid is feeling a bit lonely."

"I'm sorry to hear that. If you feel the need to go look for her, please feel free to do so."

She nodded. "Maybe I should. Sure you don't mind?"

"Mind? I insist. You've prepared a fine supper and our favorite radio program comes on in twenty minutes. Bertie and I enjoy listening to Edgar Bergen. I'm sure the little darlin's fine, but I know it'll ease your mind to have her inside before it gets any later."

Dabney grabbed a sweater and ran out the door, calling Alex's name. She ran down the road for a couple of miles, maybe further, but the child was not in sight. She threw her hand over her heart when a thought came to her. *Of course. She's inside the church. No doubt went to pray and fell asleep on a pew.* But when Dabney opened the door of the church, her heart sank. Where could she be? It wasn't like Alexandra to worry her this way. Something dreadful must've happened to her.

She ran back to the parsonage. "Brother Charlie, I couldn't find her. May I use your telephone to make a long-distance call?

You can take it out of my pay."

"Oh, sugar, you're free to use our phone anytime. Call anyone you need to. Bertie and I have prayed, and I know that God's going to protect our little Alex, wherever she is."

Dabney only wished she could have as much faith as the preacher did at this moment, but she had a gut feeling that something terribly wrong was going on. She grabbed the telephone and said, "Operator? Operator! I'd like to make a long distance call to Goat Hill, Alabama. 74-J, Person-to-Person to Mr. Oliver Weinberger."

"I'm sorry, Miss, but that line is busy. Please try again, later."

Chapter Twenty-Five

Oliver clenched the receiver until his hand felt numb. "You did the right thing, to call me, Lizzie. I'll get in touch with the police and make a report."

"Oh, Oliver, do you really think that's necessary? I only called you because I knew you'd know how to get in touch with Dabney, to let her know not to worry. Alexandra is fine. I'm sure poor Dabney must be frantic by now."

"Yeah, well . . . I need to hang up now. I'll call you back after I call the authorities."

Lizzie peeked in the parlor, where Alexandra had fallen asleep on the divan. If only Kiah were here, but he'd gone to the auction in Montgomery to buy a new hay-baler. She didn't expect him back before tomorrow.

In less than ten minutes, a policeman was knocking on the door, and Oliver was with him.

The officer said, "Ma'am, I understand there's a juvenile

runaway here? I'd like to speak with her, if you don't mind."

"Well, I do mind. She's sound asleep and I'd rather not awaken her. She was exhausted when she arrived."

"I understand your concern, but I must speak with her. However, no need to wake her yet. I have questions that I'd like you to answer for me."

"I'll do what I can, but I don't know that I'll be much help. All I know is that she showed up on my doorstep, tired and hungry."

"Did she tell you why she'd come to you?"

"No." Lizzie's eyes squinted as she attempted to remember exactly what Alexandra said. "Well, maybe she did, now that I think about it."

"Please. Anything you can recall could be important."

"She said she'd run away and that she hated Goose Hollow. That's all. I really didn't question her, she seemed so distraught." She glanced at Oliver. "I suppose Mr. Weinberger has already told you that she lives there with her nursemaid, Dabney Foxworthy."

"Did she give you any reason to suspect Miss Foxworthy had physically abused her?"

"Heavens no. Dabney loves that little girl. She would never do anything to harm her."

Oliver stepped up. "Lizzie, as your attorney, I advise you to let me answer any further questions."

The policeman said, "Thank you, Mrs. Grave. Now, if I could speak to the child."

Lizzie shook Alex gently. "Sweetheart, wake up. There's a

nice man here who'd like to ask you a few questions."

She rubbed her eyes and sat up, just as the officer and Oliver entered the room. "Oliver. I didn't know you were coming here tonight." Her gaze fixed on the policeman. "Why is he here? Is it against the law to run away? Am I gonna get arrested?"

The officer shook his head. "No. You aren't in any kind of trouble. I just rode over with Mr. Weinberger to ask you a few questions. You don't mind, do you?"

She looked at Oliver, and her fears appeared to diminish. "I don't reckon. Whatcha wanna know?"

"I understand you ran away from home. Is that right?"

"No sir."

Lizzie raised her brow. "Alexandra?"

She shrugged. "I said I ran away, but not from home. That's *not* my home."

The officer knelt down beside her. "Then where *is* your home?"

"I don't have one."

Oliver stepped up. "Honey, if you had a home, where would you like for it to be?"

"That's easy. Here."

He turned to the policeman. "Well, I think she's answered your questions. Could I speak with you outside, sir?"

The two men walked into the antechamber. Oliver said, "I think it's in the best interest of the child to leave her here in the custody of her father and his wife. You can contact the nursemaid

185

at this number." He scribbled Brother Charlie's telephone number on a slip of paper. If we're through here, I'll drive you back to the station."

Chapter Twenty-Six

Dabney tried four times before being able to get through to the police station. When an officer finally answered, she burst into tears. "My . . . my daughter's missing."

"Ma'am, I'm sorry. I'm having a problem understanding you. Who did you say was missing?"

"My daughter. She went for a walk after school and never returned. I've looked everywhere."

"Has she ever run away before?"

"Run away? Oh, no. She'd never run away. I'm terrified that she's been abducted."

"Did she have an argument with you or your husband before she went for a walk?"

"I don't have a husband, and no we didn't argue. Please, could you save the questions until after you search for her? She's only ten years old. I'm so frightened."

"Was she upset about anything?"

"Maybe, but she's a kid. Kids have a tendency to dramatize."

"So, you're saying she had a problem. Would you mind telling me about it?"

"This is ridiculous. I'm talking on the phone when I should be out searching for her. I'm sorry I wasted your time."

"Hold on. The lieutenant has just walked in and laid a report on my desk. Is the child you're calling about, ten years old?"

"Yes. I told you that earlier. Weren't you listening?"

"Ma'am, I think we've located her, but unless you calm down, we won't know for sure. Now, tell me what she was upset about."

"We recently moved from Goat Hill to Goose Hollow, and it seems she hasn't been able to make friends. You know how dramatic children can be. She came home saying she hated her school, but that's all there was to it. She gets over things quickly. She's probably already forgotten why she was so upset."

"Is her name Alexandra Grave?"

She swallowed hard. Why go into Alex's life history to clear up her last name. Evidently that was the name she gave the authorities. "That's her. You found her? Is she okay?"

"Yes ma'am, she's fine."

"Where is she? How did she get there? Will you be bringing her home?"

"She's at the home of her father, Mr. Hezekiah Grave in Goat Hill. She's chosen to stay there tonight."

"No. She can't. She has to go to school tomorrow."

"I'm sorry, ma'am, but you can hire a lawyer tomorrow and

188

work this out in court. Your daughter is alive and well. That should bring you comfort for now."

****

Dabney needed someone to blame, so she chose Oliver. It was all his fault. If he hadn't made her fall in love with him, she'd still be working for his mother, and as difficult as the woman was to work for, it was a good job with good pay. But Oliver couldn't leave well enough alone. He moved her off to the backwoods to a primitive cottage. She stayed from daylight 'til dark taking care of Mrs. Bertie, and then returned to the drafty old cabin to sleep on a ratty cotton mattress at night. It was fine as long as she thought she'd be sharing it with him. The knot in her throat swelled. What good did it do to blame Oliver?

She loved Brother Charlie and Mrs. Bertie, but she didn't make enough money working there to provide for herself, much less Alexandra. The tears streamed down her face. She'd trusted Oliver when he said he'd take care of them. What a mess she'd made of things. How could she blame Alex for running away, when she'd like to do the same thing?

Dabney cried herself to sleep.

The next morning, she told Brother Charlie she needed to take the day off to go bring Alex back.

She blew out a sigh of relief when the old car started on the third try. She drove straight to the Gladstone mansion, ran up the steps and rang the doorbell.

When the maid came to the door, Dabney said, "I'd like to see Lizzie."

"I'm sorry ma'am but Miz Lizzie, well, she ain't here. She done gone to enroll the child in school."

"What? She can't do that. Alexandra is not her child and furthermore, she's coming back with me."

"Yes'm. If you say so. But I spect you need to clear that with Miz Lizzie."

"May I come in and wait for her?"

"I done been told not to let nobody inside who comes asking about the young'un. I reckon that'd be you."

"This is insane. Alexandra doesn't belong to her. Why would she say such a thing?"

"T'weren't her what said it. It was Mr. Kiah's lawyer, what left the instructions."

"His *lawyer*?"

Chapter Twenty-Seven

If Dabney had to eat crow, she would, even if it choked her. She pulled up in front of Oliver's house and walked around to his office door and knocked.

"Door's open. Come on in," he shouted. His eyes widened. "Oh. It's you."

"Yes, it's me. What's going on, Oliver? Why are you acting this way? What did I do to make you so angry at me?"

"I see we're back to Oliver. Not Kip? Gee whiz, Dabney, I guess it was just too difficult to turn a mule into a race horse."

"Please. I'm sorry I even asked. Whatever we had going on between us is over. I get it. But at the moment, that's not my greatest concern. I came because I need you. Your services, I mean. I don't have any money, but I'll get it somehow, if I have to work two jobs day and night. Please, Oliver. You've gotta help me." Her lip quivered. "Alexandra's run away."

He glared in silence.

"Didn't you hear what I said? Jeepers, Oliver, even if you hate me, I thought you cared about Alex. Don't you want to know when? Why? You act as if you don't care."

"Why should I be concerned? We both know she's perfectly safe with Eliza and Kiah."

"So you've heard?" Rolling her eyes, she said, "I don't know why I'm surprised, the way gossip travels around here. Well, did you also know that Lizzie and Kiah have hired a lawyer and I have a feeling they're gonna try to get custody of Alex?"

The leather swivel chair squeaked when Oliver rotated around. Gazing out the window, he said, "Though it isn't my place to be giving you advice . . . if I were to, I'd advise you to do the same. That is, if you really want to get Alexandra."

Dabney's jaw dropped. "What do you mean *if* I really want her? She belongs with me, and I'm here because I want you to represent me."

"I'm afraid that's impossible. I'm representing the Graves. And as their attorney, you and I have nothing further to discuss."

Tears clouded her eyes. "What? Why, Oliver? Why are you doing this to me? Even if your mother has convinced you I'm not worthy of your love, don't you have enough compassion in your heart for Alex? Imagine the trauma of jerking her away from me . . . the only 'mama' she's ever really known?"

He trudged over to the door, opened it and stood there expressionless, looking like a wax mannequin. With his hand, he gestured toward the outside. "Good day, Miss Foxworthy. We'll see you in court."

****

192

Driving home, Dabney could hardly see for the tears clouding her vision. If only she hadn't come looking for Kiah, none of this mess would be happening. So she made Zann a promise. But how long was one expected to keep a promise to a dead person? Didn't she realize there was a possibility Kiah might use Zann's words to snatch Alexandra away from her? "No, no! I never expected this. I thought—" She gripped the steering wheel so tightly, her hands turned white. She knew exactly why she came to Goat Hill, though she didn't want to admit it. *I dreamed Kiah would be single, he'd fall in love with me, and we'd become one happy little family—me, Kiah and Alexandra.* The delightful fantasy had turned into a horrid nightmare.

Brother Charlie was sitting on the porch swing when she drove up. He looked up from the book in his lap. Though she tried to hide the tears, she supposed it was the bloodshot eyes and red, runny nose that gave her away.

He said, "I take it things didn't go your way, today."

Dabney burst into full-blown sobs. "Oh, Brother Charlie, they're trying to take her away from me. They've hired a lawyer."

"I'm sorry that you're so distraught, sugar. Come sit beside me and let's pray for God to work this situation out for everyone's good and His glory."

Dabney balked. For *everyone's* good? How could she possibly approach God with such an impossible request? Someone was bound to get hurt, and she knew exactly who she wanted that to be and it wasn't her or Alexandra. "I'm sorry, preacher, I can't.

193

Doesn't the Bible tell us that God will give us the desires of our heart? Well, that's what I plan to pray for. *My* desires, not theirs. And my desire is for Kiah and Lizzie to send Alexandra back where she belongs. With me. She's not Kiah's or Lizzie's child and I won't allow them to take her from me."

"Yes, child, the Bible does indeed say that God will give us the desires of our heart, but the first part of that verse says for us to delight ourselves in the Lord. Don't you think it delights the Lord when we acknowledge that we completely trust Him with everything that's dear to us? You're correct in saying that Alexandra isn't their child, but neither is she yours. She belongs to God. Let's ask Him to help us line up our desires with His. Are you ready to pray that prayer?"

She shook her head. "No sir. I can't."

"Why not, child?"

"Because I'm afraid."

"Afraid of talking to God?"

"Afraid that I can't honestly pray for God to line my prayer up with his desire, because in my heart I'm terribly frightened that He'll choose Lizzie and Kiah over me. Why wouldn't He? They're married and can provide things for her that I can't. I get it. But Alex and I belong together. The Graves can't possibly love her as much as I do. I couldn't go on living if they should take her from me. Brother Charlie, do you happen to know a good lawyer?"

He reared back and chuckled, though Dabney saw nothing humorous in the question. "Did I say something funny?"

194

"I'm sorry, sugar. We only have one lawyer in Goose Hollow, and I understand he's a cracker-jack lawyer. They say he knows his business and wins most of his cases."

"So why did you laugh?"

"Because you asked about a *good* lawyer. I've never heard Dave Whigham referred to as being good. He seems to delight in his colorful bad boy reputation." A wry smile crept across his face. "But then I've always believed there was a little bad in the best of us and a little good in the worst of us. So I'm sure if anyone can find the good in Mr. Whigham, it'll be you."

"His reputation makes no difference to me. I don't plan on marrying the fellow. Dave Whigham, you say? Thanks, Brother Charlie."

"Just be careful, sugar. He's swept more than one woman off her feet, although it's beyond me how he manages to woo them. I understand he's just finalized his third divorce. I reckon that sounds like idle gossip but it's not meant to be. I just feel the need to warn you to tread softly. I have a feeling this could be a very vulnerable time in your life, and I want you to be cautious."

"I appreciate your concern, preacher, but I'm in no position to be choosy. I need a good lawyer and if he'll let me pay him on 'time,' then I'll hire him."

The following morning, Dabney paced back and forth in front of Dave Whigham's office, waiting for him to arrive. Though she'd practiced her speech most of the night, her thoughts scrambled, the moment he stomped into the waiting room.

His secretary said, "Mr. Whigham, Miss Foxworthy is here to see you." Without as much as glancing her way, he mumbled incoherently while chewing on a cigar, walked into the next room and slammed the door. The secretary shuffled through a few papers, looked up, and as if irritated that Dabney didn't follow him in, she said, "I wouldn't keep him waiting if I were you."

"He's ready to see me?"

The prune-faced woman looked up and scowled. "We don't send out engraved invitations."

"I apologize. I . . .I didn't understand. Should I knock?"

Rolling her eyes, the woman said, "Open the door. He's waiting, but Dave Whigham doesn't wait long for anyone, so I advise you to either go in or go out."

"Yes ma'am. Sorry."

Dabney cracked the door open slightly, giving just enough time to let him know she was entering. Then pushing the door open, her heart pounded so fast she felt she might faint. "Mr. Whigham?"

He reared back in his swivel desk chair, eyed her from head to foot, then grinned. "Well blow me down. So you're Miss Foxworthy?"

"Yessir." Dabney wrung her hands together.

"Well, come on in and take a seat, sugar. Had I known such a lovely lady was waiting for me, I would've been here an hour ago." He picked up a pen and scribbled something on a pad.

"What's your first name, Miss Foxworthy?"

"Dabney, sir. That's with a 'B'."

"Babney?"

Dabney flinched. "No sir. Dabney. Most folks think I'm saying Daphne, like Daphne Du Maurier."

"Daphne du who?"

She shrugged. "Doesn't matter."

"No, I'm interested. Daphne is a very unusual name. I like it."

"But it's not *my* name. My name is Dabney. With a 'B'." She bit her tongue. *How stupid that sounded.* When it appeared he was waiting for her to explain, she said, "Daphne Du Maurier wrote the book, Rebecca. Maybe you saw the move at the Avon Theatre a couple of weeks ago, starring Joan Fontaine and Laurence Olivier."

He chuckled.

"What's funny, sir?"

"I was wondering why you asked if I'd seen the picture show but you didn't ask if I'd read the book. Maybe I look like someone who can't read."

Her face twisted into a frown. "Oh, no sir. That's not at all what I was inferring."

"Just jawin' with you. But to answer your question, no I didn't see the movie. So, Dabney, with a 'B'—do you mind if I call you Dabney?"

She swallowed hard. "Please do." After going through lengthy small-talk about everything from the mama cat and kittens under

197

the office porch—to the price of light bread—to President Roosevelt's funeral, Dabney's rigid body began to relax and she settled comfortably into the overstuffed leather chair. "I can't tell you how much it means to me that you'd agree to see me, Mr. Whigham."

"Sweetheart, you can't imagine what a treat it is to sit here and *see* you. You're a sight for sore eyes. I bet you have a lot of beaus, pretty as you are."

Reminding herself that Dave Whigham was her only hope, Dabney ignored the comment and plunged ahead with the script she'd practiced for hours before coming. "Though I don't have any money at the present, I promise to begin paying you as soon as I can find a better job."

He smiled. "I can see I've embarrassed you. I shouldn't have joked around like that. Most people in town know I carry on foolishness, but I realize you don't know me. So if I offended you, please forgive me."

His voice was gentle and kind, yet she had the distinct impression that the same soothing tone could become instantly antagonistic and gruff if riled. She needed this man. He was her only hope; therefore, she vowed not to ruffle his feathers, regardless of what she had to endure to stay on his good side.

"That's okay, Mr. Whigham."

"Call me Dave." He snuffed out the cigar in a large ashtray and tossed it into a brass cuspidor. "And I'm not worried about the money. I'm a good judge of character and I know we'll be able to work something out that'll be satisfactory to both of us. You apparently have bigger problems at the moment, so we'll talk money after we get this case closed. I think you'll find me exceptionally easy to work with."

Dabney went through the whole rigmarole . . . about how she pretended to be pregnant after the preacher's daughter was raped, so the parishioners in Reverend Pruitt's church would think she, and not Zann, was the baby's mother. "I did it to protect Zann. She was such a good girl and what she went through was horrible. If people had known she had a baby, it could've given her a bad name, ya' know?"

His brow furrowed. "Forgive me for sounding naive, but why would you damage your own good name for the sake of someone else?"

She glanced down and twisted a handkerchief in her hands. "I'm ashamed to tell you, Mr. Whigham."

"Dave!"

She nodded. "Yess'r. Truth is, I didn't have a good name. I reckon you might say I was the town's dirty joke. So I thought if I could save Zann from the kind of stares I got every day, then it'd be the only good thing I'd ever done in my whole life."

Dabney's face burned. *Stupid, stupid, stupid!* This wasn't the scenario she'd so carefully rehearsed. What did her past reputation have to do with getting Alexandra back? Why not get up and leave now, to save him from having to embarrass them both? He'd conclude he wasn't as good at judging character as he wanted to believe.

Dave reached in his desk drawer and took out a small cedar box. He pulled out a cigar, bit off the end, then lit it with a fancy lighter. Rearing back in his chair, he said, "You sweet thing. How many young women would go to such lengths for a friend? What I'd give to find such a loyal friend before I die. You're a very special person, Dabney Foxworthy."

Dabney's pulse slowed. "And you're a nice man, Mr. Whig . . . uh, Dave. I reckon most big time lawyers like yourself would've tossed me out on my ear, after hearing about my shameful past."

"To the contrary. I admire you even more for telling me the truth." He looked at his watch. "Let's you and I go to lunch over at City Cafe, and we can finish our discussion there."

She jumped up. "Oh my goodness, is it that late? I need to get back and prepare lunch for my employer and his wife. I had no idea I'd been here that long."

"Then tonight?"

"I beg your pardon?"

"I know where the preacher lives. I'll pick you up at five o'clock. I'd like to know everything there is to know about your case, and there's no reason we can't mix business with pleasure."

"Could we make it six-thirty? I have chores to do and I couldn't possibly be done by five."

"Six-thirty it is."

Chapter Twenty-Eight

When the school bell rang, Alexandra ran out the door, holding hands with a rather bedraggled looking, barefoot little girl. When Alex spotted Lizzie waiting for her, she turned loose and ran toward the car.

Lizzie said, "Hi, hon. Who's your friend?"

"Her name's Nelda Sue. Her mother is Mrs. Weinberger's wash woman. Nelda Sue's my best friend in the whole world."

"I see. So, you're happy to be back in school here?"

"Yes'm. I didn't have any friends at Goose Hollow. Maybe Dabney will move back. I think she and Oliver had a fight but if you ask me, she still loves him and I think he loves her. I may be a kid, but I can just tell about things like that."

Lizzie smiled. "You love Dabney a lot, don't you?"

"Sure. Did you call and tell her where I am? Is she mad at me for running away?"

"She knows you're with us, sweetheart. And I'm sure she

understands."

"I hope she'll let me stay with you and Kiah so I can go to school here with my friends. Did she say if I can stay? Wouldn't it be swell if she could move in with us? She can sleep with me in my room and she's a swell cook. She's a good housekeeper, too."

Lizzie swallowed hard. "There are a lot of details that have to be worked out, but nothing that should concern you. It's adult stuff. We'll talk about it later. Guess what? I bought you a few new clothes today. I hope you like them. Look in the bags in the back seat and see what you think."

Alex grabbed a large shopping bag from the back and pulled out one outfit after another. "Jeepers creepers, these are for me?"

"Well, I don't think they'd fit me. Do you like them?"

"*Like* them? These are the most beautiful clothes I've ever seen." From the bottom of the last bag, she pulled out a pair of white silk pajamas and a shiny red satin house coat. She slid over and snuggled close to Lizzie. "You're swell, Lizzie. Nobody's ever done anything like this for me. Nobody. Thank you."

"I'm so glad you like them, sweetheart. How does a big chocolate malt sound?"

"Really? You know how to make malted milks? My grandfather bought me one once and it was really, really good."

"I don't make them, but I know where we can buy one. Pop Jackson's Drug Store makes the best I've ever tasted."

Lizzie had never seen anyone consume a large malt in such a

short length of time. "Doesn't your head hurt?"

"It does, but it was worth it. When will Kiah be home?"

"Oh, he's there now. He walked in the door as I was leaving to pick you up."

"Was he surprised when you told him I'm living with you?"

"I was already in the car and didn't have time to tell him."

"You think he'll be surprised?"

"I'm sure he will, honey."

When Lizzie walked into the house with Alex, a wide smile stretched across Kiah's face. "Alexandra! What a nice surprise. Where's Dabney?"

"She's still in Goose Hollow."

His brow creased. "But what are you . . . I mean why . . ."

Alex turned toward Lizzie and grinned. "I live here now."

He laughed. "Oh, you do, do you? Well, that sounds like a great idea to me. Whatcha got in the bag?"

"New clothes Lizzie bought for me. Wanna see?"

Reading the confusion on her husband's face, Lizzie said, "Alexandra, honey, you can show him later. Why don't you run upstairs and put them in your room."

Lizzie waited for Alex to get out of sight. "It's a long story, Kiah. I don't even know where to begin."

His eyes darkened. "Start anywhere. I'll try to keep up. What did she mean, she's living here? Where's Dabney? And exactly what did you mean when you told her to put her clothes in *her* room?"

"Slow down, Kiah, and I'll answer all your questions, one at the time."

After sitting through an abbreviated explanation, he said, "Honey, Alexandra is just a kid. She isn't old enough to make these kind of decisions. We need to sit her down, talk with her and let her know that we understand that it's sad to leave old friends and it takes time to make new ones. We have to take her back where she belongs. She's a friendly little girl. She'll adjust quickly."

"Kiah, don't you get it? She *is* where she belongs. You didn't go looking for Dabney, she came looking for you. And why? Because she made a promise to her friend that if the grandparents weren't able to raise Alexandra, that she'd bring her to you. No one forced her to do that. If she'd really wanted the child, she wouldn't have brought her here. She did it because she wants you to have Alexandra."

He rubbed his chin. "When you say it like that, it does appear that she expected me to take Alex, but it's hard to comprehend. Dabney's crazy about the kid."

"Well, of course, she is, but think about it, Kiah. She's losing her youth and fast becoming an old maid, so she has her own happiness to consider. Finding a husband becomes even more difficult when you add a child to the equation."

"But I've never known Dabs to put her own needs first."

"If you ask me, she's putting Alexandra's needs ahead of her own. I'm sure Dabney realizes you're in a much better position to care for Alex than she is. Honey, don't you see? This is the answer to prayer. I'd just gone to Oliver that morning to inquire as to what steps we'd need to take to adopt her, and then she shows up at our door. Now, tell me, that's not divine intervention."

"Whoa! Adopt her? You mean you took it upon yourself to discuss adoption with a lawyer, even *before* Alex arrived?"

"Exactly! And when I saw her standing there in the doorway, looking so forlorn, it was all the confirmation I needed that I'd done the right thing."

Alexandra walked to the edge of the top of the stairs, in time to hear Lizzie say, "Think about it, Kiah. Dabney came here for one purpose only, but she didn't want to look like a bad person for giving Alex up. So I reasoned it'd be easier for her if we went ahead and initiated the proceedings. I took the birth certificate with me, and Oliver assured me he'd take care of all the details."

When Kiah leaned his head back, Alex hurried back into the bedroom. *So Dabney doesn't want me?* A part of her wanted to sneak back out, yet another part warned her not to eavesdrop. She'd already heard more than she wanted to know.

"I thought you'd be happy, Kiah. Don't you want her?"

"Well, of course, Lizzie . . . but we can't just take her away from Dabney."

"We aren't taking her away. We're *accepting* her because it was her mother's dying wish. Surely, that means something to you.

205

She trusted you, Kiah."

"Lizzie, you did explain to Oliver that even though my name's on the birth certificate, that I'm not the father, didn't you?"

"Oh, I didn't have to explain anything. Dabney had already told him the whole story. He's sweet on her. Did you know that? Isn't that cute?" She giggled. "Who would've ever expected those two to get together? What an unlikely pair."

"I don't get it. You say he's representing us, yet he's in love with Dabney?"

"Unusual, for sure. Maybe they were waiting for us to make the first move, to make sure we wanted Alexandra."

"So let me see if I've got this straight. After talking to Oliver Monday morning about the possibility of adopting Alex, the kid just happens to show up at our door that evening?"

"How many ways do I have to say it, Kiah? Don't you believe me? When I opened the door, I gasped. The poor little darling looked like a ragamuffin standing there. She said she rode in the back of a poultry truck to get here and was starving. I didn't know what to do, so I called Oliver because I knew he'd know how to get in touch with Dabney. I wanted to do the right thing."

"What did Dabney say?"

"I haven't spoken with her."

"What!? For crying out loud, Liz, you mean all this took place two days ago and you still haven't contacted Dabney?"

"Stop yelling at me. If you'd been here, you could've helped make the decisions that had to be made, but you weren't here, were

206

you?"

He reached over and wrapped his arms around her. "Sorry, hon. I'm just trying to imagine how Dabs must be feeling."

Her eyes watered. "Your first concern is for Dabney? What about me, Kiah? Aren't you even a little interested in how I'm feeling? Or don't I matter to you?"

"Oh, sweetheart, I'm sorry if I hurt your feelings. Of course you matter more to me than anyone. I'm just having a hard time sorting all this out." He reached over and took her hand in his. "Finish."

She snubbed and dried her tears. "Well, as I was about to say before you started yelling at me, I called Oliver and asked how I could reach Dabney."

"So Oliver called her?"

"Uh . . . first he called the police."

"The police? But why?"

"He said it was his duty to report a runaway."

Kiah nodded. "Well, of course. I'm sure Dabney must've already reported her missing and Oliver needed to let them know she was safe."

Lizzie shrugged. "Maybe."

"Liz, is there something you aren't telling me? You seem very evasive."

"No. For goodness sake, Kiah, don't you trust me? I've told you everything, exactly the way it happened. I went to Oliver Monday morning to inquire about adoption and he said there'd be a custody hearing, but not to worry, he'd handle everything. Then Alexandra showed up that evening and I called Oliver because I didn't know how to reach Dabney. He alerted the authorities, they quizzed Alex, and she told them she wanted to stay here." Lizzie lifted her shoulders in a dismissive shrug. "Who knows? Maybe the little thing sensed Dabney needed her freedom."

"Go on. I'm having a hard time making sense of all this."

"It's all quite simple, really. So yesterday, I enrolled her in school and today I bought her some clothes and that's the whole story. Now, I suppose it's just a matter of time before the hearing, and she'll be ours. Can you believe it? We've got us a daughter, Kiah. And she loves us. After that last miscarriage, I've been so unhappy. I was certain I'd never know what it's like to be a mother. Now, God has given me that opportunity. I love her already, as if she were my own flesh and blood. If Alexandra looks anything like her mother, I can understand how you could've fallen in love with her. She's such a little beauty."

He swallowed hard. "She's a carbon copy of her mother. Same long black curls, same complexion, same eyes." The corner of his lip curled. "It's as if I'm looking at Zann."

Chapter Twenty-Nine

Dabney found it difficult to understand why Brother Charlie didn't seem to approve of Dave Whigham. True, he was a kidder and sometimes she didn't know how to take his jokes, but she'd never been out with anyone who was more of a gentleman.

Truth be told, she'd never really been out with anyone on a real date, other than Oliver, and though he was up on his etiquette, even he didn't go to the lengths that Dave did to treat her like a queen.

She tipped her head toward her shoulder to smell the fragrant gardenia he pinned on her blouse, though he insisted this was a working dinner, and not a date. She'd never had a store-bought corsage before.

"I simply couldn't resist when I walked by the flower shop," he said. "I know how distraught you must feel, Dabney, and I wanted to do something to lift your spirits. I hope you aren't offended."

Offended? It was such a simple gesture, but how sweet of him to be concerned about her feelings. If he treated his clients with such compassion, she wondered what it'd be like to go on a real date with the man. Not that she had any such desire. But she did wonder.

After parking the car in front of a building with a big, blinking Neon sign, he reached for her hand. With his arm crooked, Dave tucked her arm into his and led her up a flight of marble steps and into the fancy, candle-lit restaurant.

Glancing around at the women in fancy tea dresses, she swallowed hard and tugged at Dave's sleeve. She whispered, "I'm not properly dressed. I don't want to embarrass you. There's a café on Main Street. Maybe we should go there."

He leaned over and whispered in her ear. His warm breath caused prickles on the back of her neck. "Don't kid yourself. You're the most alluring woman in this room. They need the frills. You don't. You're gorgeous in anything you put on."

Maybe he meant it, maybe he didn't, but it was all that Dabney needed to make her feel beautiful in her plain calico.

The waiters were decked out in white coats and spoke with a smattering of an accent. French, she supposed. Small vases of fresh flowers were on the linen draped tables, and freshly laundered napkins were tucked inside cut-glass goblets. Soft music played on a Victrola in the corner. Dabney supposed this was what it felt like to be a Princess.

After finishing off the last bite of the baked Alaska, she said,

"I suppose we need to get down to business. What do I need to do to get Alex back?"

"You need not do a thing. Leave everything to me." He reached across the table and placed his hand on hers. "Trust me, beautiful?"

Sensing an intense interest in his low, hoarse voice, a hot flush raced across her face. She dropped her gaze, choosing to focus on their hands and not on the dark, penetrating eyes that seemed to see through her in the candle-lit room. "I do, Dave. Thank you."

"There may be a hearing before a judge, but believe me, the Graves don't have a leg to stand on. No judge is gonna take a child from you who's been your ward since the day she was born—and especially since the Child Welfare Department saw fit to leave her in your care after her grandfather died. I understand the Graves are childless and would like to have this little girl for their own, but they can't arbitrarily decide they're gonna pick a child at random and decide to adopt her. What I can't fathom is why Oliver Weinberger would've taken the case. It doesn't make sense. Ordinarily, he wouldn't touch a custody dispute."

"You . . . you know Oliver?"

"Not personally, but we've had a few run-ins."

"Run-ins?"

Dave's lip curled. "Poor choice of words on my part. But we've had several occasions to be on opposite sides of the court room. He's a good attorney. One of the best. Most of his cases are high profile, or at least considered high for our neck o' the woods.

211

That's why I'm surprised he'd concern himself with a custody case that he can't possibly win."

"I don't understand, either." She sucked in a lungful of air and prayed the tears swelling in her eyes would not roll down her cheeks. "I thought he was my friend." Her voice trembled.

Dave leaned in toward her, until she could feel his breath on her neck. "Dabney, I'm asking as your friend and not as your attorney, so don't feel an obligation to answer if you'd rather not. But I'm curious. Exactly how close a friend is he?"

Dabney chewed the inside of her cheek before deciding if she should answer. Why not? She had nothing to be ashamed of. "Oliver is the reason I left Goat Hill and moved to Goose Hollow."

Dave's eyes widened. "Really? Hmm . . . Maybe I *do* need to continue this conversation as your attorney instead of your friend. Tell me exactly what he did to make you feel you needed to get out of town."

"I didn't mean to imply he did anything sinister." Heat rose to her cheeks when she realized Dave's hand was still covering hers. Slowly she slid it out, lifted her coffee cup and took a sip. Why did she mention that Oliver had anything to do with her relocating? Now, she had an obligation to explain and it wasn't something she wished to discuss. "Dave, I worked for Mrs. Weinberger—"

"Whoa. Oliver, married? Pardon me for laughing, but when did that happen?"

"He isn't married. I meant his mother."

"Oh! I should've known. In what capacity were you

employed?"

"I was the cook."

"Are you serious? I'm sure a smart, pretty girl like you can find more suitable employment than that of a household servant." He smiled. "Forgive me, sweetheart. From the red glow on your face, I see I've embarrassed you again. My mouth seems to be faster than my brain. I'm sorry. Please continue. You were his mother's cook, so how did you and Oliver become chummy?"

She lifted a shoulder. "You're asking how? I'm not sure. I suppose it was because we were both lonely. I thought he really cared about me. Stupid, huh? Me, a cook, thinking a big-time attorney was romantically interested."

"I'm sure he gave you reason to assume such."

She nodded. "Yes, but I feel like a dope, now. I should've known better. What a laugh."

"No. It's not funny, but it's also nothing new. I'm sure he led you on. I want to know exactly what he did."

"Forget it. It's not important."

"It may be more important than you realize. Please. Take your time and don't be embarrassed."

She couldn't look him in the eyes. With her head lowered, she said, "Oliver said he wanted to marry me and that he wanted to open up a small office in Goose Hollow where he'd take pro-bono cases."

"Pro Bono? Ye gads. He told you that? What a line. Honey, you're so sweet and naïve, but that's an old trick. Naturally, once

213

he made you believe he was romantically interested, the next step would be to move you out of town so no one would become suspicious that he was having a little rendezvous with a woman outside his social circle? Am I right?"

She bit her lip and nodded. "Yes, that's exactly what he did. He rented a little log cabin and moved me in it. I received one letter from him, and then there were no more letters, no phone calls—nothing. And now, he's representing the people who are trying to take Alex from me, and no one knows better than Oliver how much I love that little girl."

"What a jerk. Well, he won't get away with it. We'll sue for breach of contract."

Dabney's jaw dropped. "No! Please, Dave. Don't go there. I'd be humiliated. All I want is for you to get Alexandra back. I want to forget I ever knew Oliver Weinberger."

Chapter Thirty

Dabney called Dave Friday morning. "Dave, I'm going crazy. What's going on? Alexandra has been gone five days, and that's five more days of missed school. The longer she stays in Goat Hill, the harder it's gonna be for her to catch up and adjust."

"I was planning to call you today. Judge Martin has set up a hearing for the fifteenth of next month." After a long pause, he said, "Dabney? You still there?"

"I'm here. I can't believe what I've just heard. That's three weeks away. Dave, that's not acceptable. Doesn't that judge know she needs to be in school?"

"That's the thing, Dabney. She *is* in school, but it's the school she wants to go to."

She screamed into the receiver. "Alexandra is a child. She doesn't get to make decisions on a whim. I'm going to Goat Hill and talk sense into Kiah. He can't do this."

"That's inadvisable, Dabney. If you want Alex back, don't

make contact with the Graves. It could throw a cog in the wheel. I know this is distressing, but we have to wait for the hearing. After that, you shouldn't ever have to worry about losing her again."

****

Alexandra jumped out of bed at the crack of dawn, Saturday morning. She ran into Kiah and Lizzie's bedroom and jumped up on the bed and bounced. "Time to wake up, you sleepyheads."

Kiah grabbed her and tickled her until she could hardly catch her breath. "You little stinker, what are you doing waking up at daylight? I haven't even heard the rooster crow yet."

"You said we'd go to the beach today. I've never been to the beach. Can we go now? Wake up Lizzie."

Lizzie turned over and smiled, seeing Alex in the pink polka-dotted swimsuit she bought her from Blumberg's. It was even cuter on her than Lizzie had imagined. *What a perfect child.* "I'm awake, Punkin'. Why don't you run on downstairs while we get dressed? You can tell Cleo what you'd like for breakfast."

"I want blueberry pancakes. She makes them almost as good as Dabney's."

Lizzie felt a lump form in her throat. She hated these feelings of jealousy that cropped up out of nowhere. She had no reason to be jealous of Dabney Foxworthy. After all, she had everything Dabney had ever wanted. She had Kiah, a beautiful home, financial security and now they had Alexandra. If anyone should be jealous, shouldn't it be Dabney?

Cleo's eyes widened when Alex ran into the kitchen. "Guess what, Cleo! We're gonna go swimming."

Lizzie and Kiah walked through the door, arm-in-arm. "That's right, but you need to go wash your hands and get to the table. Cleo must be a mind-reader. She has the blueberry pancakes made already."

Alex giggled. "She knows they're my favorite, don't you Cleo?"

The elderly black lady wiped her hands on a dishrag, then plopped one hand on her hefty hip, and with her other hand, wagged her index finger in the direction of Lizzie and Kiah. "Y'all ain't really gonna take that young'un to no beach on a day like this, I hope. It ain't fittin' weather to go a'swimmin' in. And that ain't all—"

Kiah glanced over and winked at Lizzie. "It never is, Cleo."

"Well, I'm just sayin' Alice has been runnin' around all over the place for days, barefooted as a yard dog. Ever'body knows little young'uns ought not to be pulling off their shoes 'til the first of May."

Lizzie giggled. "Her name's Alex, not Alice, but thanks for the tip, Cleo."

Kiah raised a brow. "May Day, you say? I guess I didn't read that section in the 'How to Raise a Child' manual." He playfully jerked on Cleo's apron string, untying her apron, and she promptly slapped at his hand. A ritual they went through every morning.

"Poke fun all you want, Mr. Kiah, but it's the gospel truth.

217

Po' little creature don't know no better, but you two are grown and could benefit from some plain ol' common sense. The month of March is for kite-flying, not for running around half-naked in one of them skimpy little bathing suits on a windy beach." She sat a platter of link sausage on the table. "Mark my word, she'll catch her death of cold, but I'm just batting my gums. Y'all ain't listening to a word I'm saying, and I know it. "

Kiah walked up behind her and gave her a hug. "You worry too much, Cleo. She'll be fine. She's a tough little girl."

After breakfast, Lizzie had Cleo packed a picnic lunch and Kiah, Lizzie and Alex rode down to the sandy beach in Appalachicola. Kiah had packed a fishing pole, but Alexandra was more interested in playing with the minnows in the edge of the water than trying to catch a fish with a pole. At noon, Lizzie found a vacant picnic table and Kiah grabbed the wicker basket from the backseat of the car and spread out the tablecloth. After downing fried chicken, potato salad, corn pones and blackberry tarts, Lizzie insisted Alex didn't need to go back into the water.

Alex poked out her lip and grumbled. "Why can't I swim?"

Lizzie said, "Your teeth are chattering, your lips are blue and if you need another reason, you ate a big lunch and I'm afraid you'll get cramps, sweetheart."

"No, I won't. I promise."

Kiah said, "Alex, do as your . . ." He paused.

Lizzie looked at Kiah and swallowed hard. Had he almost said, "Do as your *mother* says?" She was positive that was what he almost said before he caught himself. She found it to be bittersweet. Bitter, because she wasn't Alexandra's mother, but sweet that her precious husband already viewed her in the role of a mother. A role that she would give up Gladstone to possess.

She let out a soft sigh when he finished his sentence. "Do as you're told." So she was wrong. It was a nice thought, anyway. And one day, she'd hear her husband say those words she longed to hear: "Alexandra, do as your mother says."

Kiah and Lizzie helped Alex build a huge sand castle, complete with a moat, then gave in to her whining and allowed her to take one last dip in the ocean before gathering up their things to go.

She tuned up to cry whenever Kiah insisted it was time to leave, but before he'd finished loading the car, Alexandra was sound asleep on the back seat.

Lizzie slid up close to her husband on the way home. "Thank you, darling."

He wrapped his arm around her. "For what?"

"For such a wonderful time. We're becoming a real family, Kiah. I'm almost afraid I could be dreaming and that I'm going to wake up."

****

Saturday evening Brother Charlie walked out on the porch, where Dabney sat rocking slowly back and forth in the creaky swing. "Wishing on a star?"

Dabney looked up and forced a smile. "I would if I thought it would help. I've just been sitting here wondering what Alex has been doing today. Mrs. Bertie asleep?"

He nodded. "Sleeping like a baby. That's one more thing to be grateful for. She's able to sleep well. I wanted to come tell you how much she enjoyed the chicken and dumplings you fixed for supper. You're an excellent cook." He gazed up in the heavens when his voice quivered. "Bertie was always a good cook. I reckon that's one of the things she misses the most. She loved puttering around in the kitchen. Thanksgiving was her favorite time of the year. Our friends, Flint, his wife Harper and their three kids always came over for lunch and oh my goodness, Bertie would outdo herself." He chuckled at the memory. "I don't reckon you know the McCalls. He's the doctor, here in Goose Hollow."

"Yes, I met him right after we moved here. He was at the school giving the kids smallpox shots. I've never heard so much wailing in my life. Are the McCalls relatives of yours?"

"No, sugar, although we feel like kin. We've known Flint since he was a little tyke. His mama and daddy were members of our church, when I pastored in Birmingham. They both drowned while we were at a church picnic. So sad it was. But Bertie and I have kept our eye on him ever since, even when he had no idea we were anywhere around. Bertie and I never had kids of our own, but I reckon Flint filled that hole in my darling's heart as good as anyone could, and I'll always be grateful to him. Bertie had a lot of love to give and it would've been a crying shame to let all that overflow of love go to waste."

220

"That's sweet. I can tell how much you love her. I hope one day to find someone who loves me in that same way, and that we can have the kind of marriage you two have."

"That's my prayer for you, too, shug. You deserve a good man. But you need to be careful. Wolves often wear sheep's clothing."

She smiled. "Have someone in mind, do you?"

"I beg your pardon?"

"I get the feeling you might be referring to Dave."

He chewed on the end of a toothpick. "It's not for me to judge another human being. But if a tree bears rotten fruit, it's a pretty clear sign you need to pick from another tree. That's all I'm saying."

"Brother Charlie, I'm sure you feel you have reason to distrust him, but Dave Whigham is one of the nicest men I've ever met. He's been nothing but a gentleman, and is very considerate of my feelings. Did you know he isn't charging to represent me? Not one single penny."

He raised a brow. "And why do you suppose that is?"

"That's what I'm trying to tell you. He's that kind of person. I told him up front that I don't have any money but I'd pay him when I can, and he took me at my word. I don't think many lawyers would do that."

When the telephone rang, Dabney ran in the house, hoping to answer before the noise woke Mrs. Bertie.

"Dabney, this is Dave. I hope I'm not calling too late."

"No. What's going on?"

"That letter you mentioned—the one Alexandra's mother wrote to you. You did say that in the letter she said she was raped and thanked you for pretending to be pregnant. Is that right?"

"Yes."

"Then I need you to bring that to my office tomorrow. We're gonna need it."

"Dave, I can't. I don't know where it is."

"What do you mean? I need that letter, Dabney. Information has come to my attention that I wasn't aware of. The letter is vital. Find it."

She lay awake for hours trying to recall Zann's exact words, but there were bits and pieces missing. The part that was clear as rain was the last paragraph, outlining Zann's wishes for the care of her baby.

The doctors won't tell me, but I know I'm dying. Mother and Daddy will be the guardians of my precious baby, but should anything ever happen to them, please promise me you'll keep up with Kiah's whereabouts, and take the child to him. I know if the time should ever come, he'll take good care of our baby.
All my love,
Zann

****

Sunday morning, Dabney woke up at five o'clock to the sound of wind whipping through the cracks in the floor. The temperature had dropped overnight from eighty degrees yesterday to a cold forty-five degrees at sun-up. It was warmer outside than it was in the old log cabin. She threw a few pieces of kindling in the fireplace on top of a couple of logs and lit a fire, yet the heat seemed to reach no further than the hearth. Though she didn't have to be at work at the preacher's house until eight o'clock, she had no reason to hang around, waiting for time to leave.

Pulling up to the parsonage at six-thirty, she was stunned to see almost a dozen cars parked near the house and in the church yard. She ran up the steps and met an elderly couple walking out of the parsonage. "What's going on?"

"It's Miz Bertie, hon. She passed in the night. Doc Flint called Deacon Jemerson at four o'clock this morning and got the word out. You must be the caregiver the preacher told us about. He said his wife thought the world of you. Talked about you all the time."

Dabney's heart sank. If only she hadn't been so consumed with her own problems, perhaps she would've noticed a downward change in the sweet old lady. Now that she thought about it, Miz Bertie didn't eat much for supper last night. *She loved my meatloaf, yet she hardly touched it. What if I'd been more observant? Maybe I could've done something to save her.* The guilt was overwhelming.

Brother Charlie attempted to rise from his chair when she walked into the room, though she insisted he keep his seat. Poor man would be lost without the love of his life to care for. Dabney wondered what it would be like to live over half-a-century with

223

one's soul-mate. Surely, very few people were so privileged. She bent down to give him a hug. "I have no words to express how sorry I am, Brother Charlie."

The smile on his face and the light in his eyes took her aback. "Sorry? No, child, it's no time to be sorry. This is a day to celebrate. You see, we've been given a precious promise. It's what we've been waiting for. Longing for. My sweet Bertie has finally reached her destination. I'm gonna miss her something terrible. Ah, but we had a grand life, Bertie and me." He chuckled as if reliving past memories. "Poor as two church mice, we were, but we had what mattered most. We had a love that couldn't be matched." His gaze dropped. "I'll miss my darling for sure, but I know it won't be long until we're together again. I can't wait. What a glorious day that will be." He motioned to a lady standing in the hallway. "Lena, how about playing us a tune on the piano?"

The woman must've been ninety if she was a day, yet stooped as she was, she ambled over and took a seat on the piano stool. "What shall I play, Charlie?"

"How about "When We All Get To Heaven?""

All the activity seemed to cease at one time. The women in the kitchen preparing breakfast stopped what they were doing and walked into the living room. The men on the porch smoking cigarettes, snuffed them out and joined the group around the piano. The old lady pounded out a few chords on the ivory keys, and then, as if a Divine Choir had come down from Heaven, the voices joined together in harmony. "When we all get to Heaven, what a day, what a glorious day that will be."

All the guilt Dabney had heaped upon herself for not being there to "save" Miz Bertie disappeared. Miz Bertie didn't need saving. According to Brother Charlie, her salvation had been taken care of many years ago. A verse from John 14 came to mind. Jesus said, "*Let not your heart be troubled: ye believe in God, believe also in me. In my Father's house are many mansions: if it were not so, I would have told you. I go to prepare a place for you. And if I go and prepare a place for you, I will come again and receive you unto myself; that where I am, there ye may be also.*"

She looked around the modest room. Was it any wonder Brother Charlie's face glowed? He didn't just preach the promise, but he believed it with all his heart.

The funeral was held Monday morning, and Brother Charlie delivered a wonderful eulogy. Though the message was filled with hope, there wasn't a dry eye in the house. Her throat tightened as she watched the old man's eyes tear up, but she gathered from his words that the tears were not because Miz Bertie had gone on, but rather because he hadn't. The pianist played for a men's quartet. They sang a song called, "Will the Circle Be Unbroken?" One thing for sure, Brother Charlie and Miz Bertie had a tiny circle, but it would one day be complete. And from the looks of the preacher leaning against the pulpit, it would not be long before that day would come. After the funeral, Dabney escorted him back to the parsonage and women were already in the kitchen, pulling out bowls of food that the neighbors had brought over. Dabney stayed and helped serve the crowd that gathered to pay their condolences. After lunch, she insisted that no one would be offended if he slipped off to the bedroom and rested. He thanked everyone, and Dabney walked him to the back.

He said, "Shug, now that Bertie's gone, I won't be needing your services any longer. I'm probably gonna leave on the bus in the next week or so and go visit a friend. She lost her husband in the war, and I've had her on my mind a lot lately. I'll want to hear from you, though, so keep in touch and let me know how things are going with you and little Alexandra."

"Oh, Brother Charlie. It pains me to think of leaving you here, all alone."

"That's sweet of you, shug, but I'm never alone." He patted the chair beside him. "He's always here and He's promised to never leave me." He walked over to the pie safe and pulled out a sugar dish. Lifting the lid, he drew out several dollar bills. "Here, shug. This is to help tide you over 'til you find another job."

She pushed his hand away. "No, Brother Charlie. I can't take money from you. You've already paid me for last week's work. I'll be fine."

"Well, of course you will. But this isn't pay, sweetheart. This is a thank-you. Bertie would've wanted me to give it to you. It was her cake money."

"Cake money?"

"Yes, she sometimes baked for folks, and they'd pay her

226

whatever they could afford. Bertie never spent the money, but kept it in the sugar jar. She'd say, 'The Lord hasn't told me who I'm s'posed to give it to, so until He does, I'll keep a lid on it." He laughed a hearty laugh. "I reckon the Lord was waiting for you to come, 'cause I've no doubt this money is yours. We weren't able to pay you much, so I hope this makes up for it."

Chapter Thirty-One

Monday afternoon after the funeral, Dabney drove over to Dave's office. She pulled a coin purse from her pocket, drew out five folded bills.

"What's that for?"

"I know it's not much, Dave, but I came into some money and I want to give it to you as a down payment on what I owe you." She plopped down a five and four ones. "How much more do I owe you?"

He laughed out loud. "Put your money back into your purse. I'll let you know when the time comes. I hope you brought the letter."

Dabney shook her head. "After I gave it to Kiah to read, I distinctly remember watching him fold it up afterward. I thought I stuck it in my pocketbook, but maybe he kept it."

Dave rolled his eyes. "That's not good. Not good at all."

"Are you saying I have to have that letter to get Alex back?"

"It looks that way, but don't panic. We'll come up with something."

"Why is the letter so important?"

"Don't you know? The birth certificate proves you're the mother. The letter confirms you aren't."

She giggled. "But the birth certificate is wrong."

"I know it. And you know it. But the judge won't know it. Not unless someone gets their hands on a certain letter that proves Zann was the mother. If the only evidence brought into the Judge's chambers is a birth certificate with your name on it, then the child will be awarded back to you."

"I don't see how a bogus birth certificate could be of value. After all, Kiah's name is also listed as the father."

"And no doubt they'll try to use that. But it will only work against them. We'll go along with it and argue that, yes, he's the father, but in ten years, he's made no effort to contact the child, nor to help out in any way."

Her jaw dropped. "I can't, Dave."

"Can't? I thought you wanted the kid."

"I do want her . . . with all my heart. But the whole thing is deceptive."

Dave whirled around in his swivel chair and jumped up. "Seems to me you're more interested in the feelings of Kiah Grave than you are in getting custody of the kid. I see I've been wasting my time. Good day, Dabney."

"Please, Dave. Don't abandon me. I didn't mean to anger you. I'll do whatever you say. I can't lose her."

He sat back down. "Then find that letter."

Dabney drove to Goat Hill and pulled up in front of Goat Hill School. She scanned the playground, hoping she might see Alexandra. Her heart pounded as she walked up the concrete steps leading to the brick building. A distinguished-looking gray-haired man met her in the corridor.

"May I help you, miss?"

"Uh . . . I'm looking for a job."

"Do you have a teaching certificate?"

"No. I was thinking maybe I could work in the lunch room."

He smiled. "Do you believe in fate?"

"Fate? Not sure what that is, exactly. But I believe in prayer and I've been praying for a job."

"Well, I think your prayers have been answered. Miss Lucy turned in her resignation this morning. She's been with us since the day the school opened, but her health is quickly declining. How soon can you go to work?"

She smiled. "Where do you keep the aprons?"

The man returned her smile. "That's quick enough. Go down to the basement—that's our lunchroom—and ask for Miss Lucy. She's been very concerned about leaving us short-handed, and can tell you what to do."

When Dabney turned to walk away, he said, "You haven't asked about the pay."

"I have a job. I'll take whatever it pays. Thank you, sir."

At eleven o'clock, the first group of students filed into the basement. Dabney was assigned the job of taking up tickets. Thrilled to know that Alexandra would soon be standing in front of her, she could hardly contain her excitement. But what if Alex burst out crying and pleaded for Dabney to take her with her? It was understandable that the first couple of nights in a big fine house like Gladstone could be exciting, but Alexandra had never been one to want to stay away from Dabney for extended periods. Dabney's eyes watered as she imagined little Alex crying herself to sleep every night. How could she explain to a ten-year old that the courts had become involved and as much as she wanted them to be together, it was out of her hands?

"Dabney? Is that really you?"

Alex wrapped her arms around her waist. "You working here, now? That's swell. I can see you every day. Well, not on Saturday or Sunday, of course, but five days are better than none. I've missed you, Dabs. There's so much to tell you."

Dabney wanted to hold on and never let go. The thought crossed her mind to grab her, run to the car and never look back. "I miss you too, kid." The line kept moving, and she was soon out of sight.

That evening Dave called and she told him about her new job. "I'll be looking for a place to live, since I'll be working in Goat Hill." His reaction shocked her.

"Are you nuts? You can't be coming in contact with the subject on a daily basis. You could jeopardize our case."

231

"I don't understand why it would hurt and it helps me to just see her. It's not as if I plan to kidnap her. Besides, the preacher no longer needs me, and I need the job. Do you realize how scarce jobs are to come by?"

"I apologize for sounding harsh. I do understand your predicament. But I can help. Turn in your resignation and come to work for me."

"I don't want any favors, Dave. You've gone out of your way to help me, already."

"So it won't be favors. You can work off what you owe me for services rendered."

"I can type, but I'm not good at keeping books. I'm a quick learner, though."

"Maybe you misunderstood. I have a secretary. I don't need another. I had more like a cook in mind. Isn't that what you did for Oliver?"

"Yes, but—"

"Then it's settled. I'll send Tony Free over with a truck tomorrow to move your things out of that shack and into the barn back of my house."

"The barn?"

"Don't worry, I don't plan to make you sleep in the barn. But your room is already furnished, so we'll store your things in the barn until you're ready to get rid of them."

"I don't know, Dave. What if people don't understand what I'm hired to do?"

He chuckled. "As long as you understand, what you're hired to do, what difference does it make what other folks think?"

"I suppose it shouldn't."

"Then it's settled."

"But what about *after* the hearing, when Alex is back with me? Will she be welcome to stay here?"

"I Suwannee, Dabney, you don't know how to take one day at the time. Don't worry about tomorrow until tomorrow comes. We have enough to deal with at the present without trying to figure out the future."

"I just need to know how you feel about kids."

"Why? Is that a proposal?"

A hot flush raced through her body. "I simply meant—"

He leaned his head back and roared with laughter. "I'm sorry. I can see I embarrassed you. I know what you meant. You'll have to get used to me. I'm a kidder. Now, let's get down to *business*. Tell me word for word what was in that letter from Zann?"

"Well, she started off thanking me, and she said she tried to believe she was doing it to save her father's ministry . . . he was a preacher, you know."

"Yeah, yeah. Don't adlib. Just try to remember what she said."

"Sorry. Well, she said she really did it because she didn't want anyone to know she was raped. The gossip, you know."

"Stick to the letter."

"I am. That's what she said. She was afraid of the gossip. She told me I was the best friend she ever had. And then right at the bottom, she told me she was dying, and that her Mother and Daddy would be Alexandra's guardians, but if anything happened to them, she wanted me to take Alex to Kiah."

"Is that all?"

"Well, she did say, 'I know he'll take good care of our baby.' I found that a bit peculiar."

"Why is that?"

"Because it's not *his* baby. Why would she say 'our'?"

"Does seem a bit peculiar, doesn't it? Unless. . . "

"Unless what?"

"Unless he was the rapist."

Her eyes widened. "No. No, no, no. That's impossible."

"Are you sure?"

"One hundred percent."

"Did she tell you who raped her?"

"Not in so many words, but I know who it was."

"Okay, don't get your feathers ruffled. I'm a lawyer. I have to look at things from every perspective."

Dabney questioned her sanity. Dave didn't need a cook. He seldom ever ate at home and there was very little housekeeping, since it was a two bedroom bungalow. Certainly not enough to justify paying her to stay there. So why did he insist she move into the house with him? A more perplexing question was why did she agree?

Chapter Thirty-Two

Lizzie tapped on Alexandra's door. "Honey, it's time for supper. Come on downstairs."

"Do I have to? I'm not hungry."

"Please open the door and let's talk."

Alex slid off the side of the bed and cracked open the door. "Whatcha want?"

"I want us to sit down and talk about what's troubling you. I know you miss Dabney. Kiah and I both understand. It breaks my heart to see you so miserable. You know how much I want you to stay here, but I love you too much to watch you suffer. I've told you I'll take you back to Dabney if that's what you really want."

"But it's not what I want."

"Then what do you want?"

"I want my Granddaddy Mack. I want things to be like they were in Foggy Bottom."

"I know you miss your grandfather, sweetheart. And if I could bring them back, I would. But I can't. Please, come downstairs and have supper with Kiah and me. We're lonely when you stay locked up here in your room. Please?"

When Alex refused to look at her, Lizzie ambled down the stairs. "Kiah," she whispered. "Please see if you can reach her. We were getting along so well and now all of a sudden she's pulling away. I can't stand to see her so unhappy. I don't know what brought about the change."

"Are you saying you want to drop the custody case and send her back to Dabney?"

"Of course not. She's where she belongs. We owe it to her mother to honor her dying wish."

"Is that why you're doing this, Lizzie? Because you feel a responsibility?"

"You know better, Kiah. I could never love another child the way I love Alexandra. She's ours. But something is going on inside that pretty little head that's causing her to be unhappy. If only she'd talk to me and tell me. Maybe she'll open up to you."

He placed his hands on his wife's shoulders, pecked her on the forehead, then walked up stairs with the intent of coaxing Alexandra to come down. He wasn't sure what he said that seemed to hit a nerve, but she mumbled under her breath and stomped down the stairs as if each step pained her. Few words were spoken during the meal, though Kiah continued to press with questions that seemed to be answerable with a single word. "How was your day?"

"Fine."

"Did you play with your friend?"

"Yessir."

"I forgot her name." Long pause. "What's your friend's name?"

"Nelsue."

"I love banana pudding. What's your favorite dessert?"

"Dunno."

After supper, he suggested the three of them sit in the parlor and talk things out. "Honey, Lizzie and I want you to know that there's nothing you can't tell us. We're family now."

"Does that mean the Judge said I'll be living here?"

"The hearing isn't for ten more days, but our lawyer has assured us that there's nothing stopping you from becoming our little girl. You're okay with that, aren't you?"

After she sat tight-lipped, staring at the floor, he glanced at his wife's tear-filled eyes and tried once more. "Alex, I think I understand. You've gone through a big adjustment and you're sad. I've been there. I know what it's like to lose someone you love."

She lifted her head and her gaze locked with his. "You do?"

He glanced at Lizzie who wiped her eyes and smiled. Apparently, he had made a connection and the dialogue was now open.

"Yes I do." He rubbed at his stomach, as if experiencing the pain. "You feel all sick inside and you can't focus on anything but the one you lost. But trust me, it does get better in time, though

237

you never stop wishing they were with you. No one else can ever take their place."

"You talking about my mama, aren't you?"

His Adam's apple bobbed and he glanced at Lizzie, his face burning. "No, sweetheart, I was referring to losing my mother."

"But you did love my mama, didn't you?"

"Uh, of course, but we were very young."

"Not too young to be in love, I don't reckon."

Lizzie got up and left the room.

Kiah said, "Alex, I did love your mama, but I'd rather not talk about it in front of my wife. It makes her sad."

"Why? Because I was born?"

"Of course not. It has nothing to do with you."

"Lizzie said Oliver was gonna fix it so I can live here forever and be your little girl."

"Would you like that?"

She gave a slight shrug without answering. "Can I go back to my room now?"

Lying in bed that night, Lizzie said, "Kiah? You awake?"

"Yep. Thought you were asleep."

"No, I can't sleep. There's something I need to say and I don't know how you're going to take it."

"Honey, if it's about what Alex said about me loving her mother, please don't let that trouble you. I was only seventeen . . . just a kid. The love I felt for Zann was nothing like the love you

238

and I share. Not that I'm trying to downplay what I felt at the time, but just as she said in her final letter to me, the tide rushed in when you came into my life. You stole my heart, the first time I laid eyes on you. The day you picked me up at the train tracks and fed me that line about being a cleaning woman."

She giggled. "Not a cleaning woman . . . a Buttermilk Maid."

He laughed, reached over and pulled her close. "That's right. How could I forget? A Buttermilk Maid. Whatever made you come up with such a cockeyed story?"

"I wanted you to take an interest in me, and I knew a fellow hopping trains, carrying a bindle stick would never make a pass at a girl if he knew her father owned half the country."

"So you admit you wanted me to make a pass?"

"Naturally. I was rather brazen in my younger days. I know I gave Mother and Father fits."

Kiah laughed and snuggled closer. "You do know what goes around, comes around, don't you? What are you going to do when Alexandra turns sixteen and throws herself at some ol' boy?"

Lizzie didn't answer.

"I'll tell you what I'll do. I'll run him off with a stick." And with that he cackled as if the thought of protecting his little girl brought him joy. "Lizzie? Did you go to sleep?"

"No. I heard you, Kiah."

"You said something about needing to tell me something. What's on your mind?"

"Kiah, it's not right."

"What's not right? I was joking about chasing her beau with a stick. I'll be a good dad. You'll see."

"I know you would've been a great dad, and I wish I could've given you a child. But, Kiah, it's not right for me to steal Alexandra from Dabney."

"Steal? What are you talking about? We're not stealing her."

"Aren't we, Kiah?"

"No. She wants to be with us. You said yourself she came knocking on our door. It's not as if you went to Dabney's and grabbed her, forcing her to come live with us."

"No, but I might as well have. I tempted her with material things she's never had. It was like Christmas every morning. What child wouldn't have wanted the gifts to continue pouring in? We took her to the movies, to the beach, to the County Fair. She's had fun, but eventually these material advantages will cease to amuse, and she'll come to resent us. She'll soon realize, just as I have, that Dabney is her mother."

"But she's *not* her mother, Lizzie, no more than you are."

"I know you want to believe that, Kiah. And so did I. But it was Dabney who was willing to allow people to ridicule her for being pregnant, and then was willing to give up a life of her own. And why? To give Alexandra a life. No mother has ever sacrificed more for a child of their womb than Dabney Foxworthy has sacrificed for Alex."

"So what are you suggesting?"

"I want to drop the case and send her back where she

240

belongs."

"Oh, honey. I know how you've longed for a child, and now you've come this close to having your dream come true. Go to sleep and you'll feel differently in the morning."

"Kiah, I know this is the right thing to do."

"Sweetheart, I'm sure at the moment you believe it. But you're making a hasty decision based on the fact that Alex was pouty tonight. She's ten years old. Just a kid. They pout. They whine. They cry. But she'll get over it. She'll probably wake up in the morning, all giggles."

"First of all, it hasn't been a hasty decision. I've prayed about it for some time now, and I have complete assurance that this is the thing to do. Furthermore, she won't get over it, as you say, and neither could I if I failed to listen to the Lord."

"Lizzie, honey, are you sure?"

"I'm sure, Kiah. She belongs with Dabney. It would be cruel to pull her away. Call Oliver."

"Now?"

"Yes. I suspect it'll be the first good night's sleep I've had in several nights."

Kiah walked back into the bedroom after making the call.

Lizzie sat up in bed. "What did he say?"

"He wants to proceed."

Her face twisted into a frown. "But why? For what purpose? Didn't you tell him our decision?"

"I did, but after listening to his reasoning, I tended to agree.

241

Oliver says the hearing is not just for Alexandra's sake, nor for Dabney's, but it's for our benefit as well. He says it's already on the docket, and there's the possibility that after a few days of thinking about it, you could come to regret your decision. Then it'll be too late."

"But I won't change my mind. Kiah, I didn't make this decision on a whim. I've prayed about it for countless hours, and I can't explain it, but God has given me a peace about giving her up. It's the only right thing to do."

"Well, according to Oliver, if you still feel the same way the day of the hearing, you can always relinquish your rights at that time. Honey, I didn't want to admit it, even to myself, but I agree with you that to take her away from Dabney would be wrong. But Oliver is our attorney and I think we should take his advice and let it play out. Though he didn't say it in so many words, I have a feeling he won't present much of a case, thus allowing Dabney to be awarded custody. By going through the motions and getting a court settlement, Dabney will never have to be afraid of losing Alex to us or anyone else."

Lizzie bit her lip. "I suppose it makes sense. And it will be nice to see Dabney's face when she discovers no one can ever separate them again."

****

Every night for two weeks in a row, Sallie Belle Sellers had sat at the dinner table with Oliver and his mother, Lula. The conversation invariably led to talk about love and marriage, though it was always a two-way conversation between his mother and her pick for a daughter-in-law.

"Oliver, dear, did Sallie tell you that her college roommate just had a new baby?"

"Yes, I do believe she mentioned it a few times."

"Well, they've been married a couple of years."

"So I've heard."

Sallie took a sip of iced tea and batted her eyelashes. "I can't wait until I get married and start a family. Doesn't that sound divine, Oliver?"

Lula chimed in. "Oliver, where's your mind? Sallie asked you a question and you sit there like a knot on a log. Snap out of it."

"Sorry. What were you saying Sallie Belle?"

"I said wouldn't you like to get married?"

"Fine. Set the date." He grimaced at the screams coming from his mother and Sallie. His stomach wrenched. What had he done? Did it matter? As much as he detested Sallie Belle Sellers, she was never going to stop pestering him and he'd never be interested in any woman but Dabney, so what difference did it make? Besides, Sallie practically lived in the house with them already. She arrived before he ate breakfast every morning, and stayed until he finished dinner every night.

Lula pushed back from the table, rushed over and threw her arms around her son. "I knew you'd come to your senses. Oh, my goodness, Sallie, we have a wedding to plan."

****

When Oliver failed to show up by six o'clock that evening, Lula picked up the phone and called Judge Martin. "J.D, would you please tell my son we're waiting dinner and he needs to come home."

"I haven't seen Oliver all day, Lula."

"Then you must've been out of the office. He had court today."

"Not today. It's been quiet around here, and I've been here since early morning. A client came by earlier in the day looking for him. I have no idea where he might be. I'll be leaving shortly, but if I happen to run into him, I'll give him your message."

"Never mind. I'm sure he'll be home soon. He knows how I detest tardiness."

Chapter Thirty-Three

Alexandra tossed and turned all night. It wasn't as if she stole the letter. Was it? She'd simply looked into Kiah's attaché case to find a pencil, when she spotted it.

Maybe it was wrong of her to read it, but when she saw her mama's name at the bottom, who could blame her for being curious? Kiah, that's who. So who could she trust? She heard Lizzie tell Kiah that Dabney wouldn't have brought her here if she wasn't trying to get rid of her. Well, not in those same words, but that's how Alex interpreted it. Then Kiah had said he didn't want her. At least that's what he meant when he said, "Lizzie, we can't just take Alex away from Dabney. It wouldn't be right." Alex stuffed her fist to her mouth to silence the sobs. He was her father. What wasn't right about a daddy wanting his little girl to be with him? There were too many secrets. Was anyone telling her the truth? Every time she walked into a room, it became quiet.

Saturday morning Alex awoke to the smell of bacon frying

downstairs. She ambled down the stairs and plopped down at the breakfast table. Cleo sat a plate of flapjacks in front of her, and said, "I declare if you ain't about the prettiest little girl I ever did see."

"They say I look like my mama, but I don't even know if that's true."

"Lawsy, child, who put that burr in yo' britches?"

Lizzie said, "Thank you for breakfast, Cleo. It looks wonderful. Now, you can be excused."

Kiah and Lizzie exchanged glances. He nodded as if to say, "You go first."

Lizzie unfolded her napkin and placed it in her lap. "Alexandra, sweetheart, what would you like to do today. Shall we go shopping? I saw the cutest pair of patent leather Mary Jane's in the show window at Holmes."

Alex shook her head. "No thanks. Don't feel like shopping."

"Is there something else you'd rather do?"

"Not really. May I be excused?"

"But you've hardly touched your food."

"Not hungry. I wanna go outside and play."

Kiah reached for his wife's hand and nodded. "Sure kid. Grab your coat. It's a bit nippy out. Don't wander off too far."

Lizzie's eyes welled with tears when the screen door slammed shut. "Kiah, my heart breaks for her. She was so giggly when she came here, and now look at her. No child should be as miserable as she seems to be. If only I could know what's going on inside her

246

little head."

"Honey, she doesn't know where she belongs. I think that's what's so troubling to her. She loves Dabney but she also loves us. Poor kid feels torn."

"Are you sure we're doing the right thing by not insisting that Oliver drop the case? I can't stand to see her so despondent. I want to let her know she doesn't have to make a choice . . . that we understand her place is with Dabney."

"I would agree with you, except I fear she might falsely conclude that we don't love her if we simply tell her we've decided she needs to live with Dabney. By having the hearing, she'll know she's loved by all of us, and after the judge's decision, we'll make sure she understands that we want to continue to have a relationship with her."

"What if you're wrong, Kiah, and the judge awards Alex to *us*?"

"We'll cross that bridge when we get there. But you've said that God has given you a peace about giving her up. Why would God give you a peace about giving her up, if she was going to continue living here?"

"I suppose you're right. I just hope Dabney will allow us the privilege of having a relationship with Alex, but I wouldn't blame her if she chose not to."

"She won't deny us that opportunity."

"How can you be sure?"

"I know Dabney. She'll fight tooth and nail for that little girl, but only when it's in Alex's best interest. And she'll know in her heart that no child can be loved by too many people." He reached over and with his index finger, stopped a tear from sliding down Lizzie's cheek. "I love you so much, sweetheart. You've talked about the sacrifices Dabney has made for Alex's sake. But I happen to know that this decision is a giant sacrifice on your part. Greater love hath no mother than this: that she lay down her life for a child."

Lizzie smiled through her tears. "If you were attempting to quote Scripture, I fear you failed. But the sentiment was lovely, anyway. Thank you."

****

Alex walked down the dirt road until she saw a little white dog run into the woods. She chased it, yet it stayed just far enough out of reach for her to pet it. "Here, puppy, here puppy," she called. But the little dog seemed to be enjoying the chase. Out of breath, she gave up and was ready to turn back, when she heard the sound of rushing water.

She walked a few steps further and looked down the bank at a beautiful flowing creek. A rope hung from a nearby tree. Alex could only imagine the fun of swinging from the rope, across the water to the other side. She stared at the width of the creek, then convinced herself she could do it. Clasping her hands around the thick roll of hemp, she stepped back several paces, then with a running start held tightly as her body sailed through the air. "I made it!" She squealed. Then looking back, she realized the rope was back on the other side of the creek. How would she manage to get back home? She walked down the edge of the bank, searching for a sturdy vine, yet there were none close enough to the water to be of help. That's when she saw an old abandoned house. *Maybe there's a rope inside.*

When she stepped on the porch, a voice called out. "Who's there?"

Alex jumped off the porch and started to run, when she heard the man call her name. "Alexandra, what are you doing out here?"

"Oliver? You scared me half to death. Do you live here?"

He laughed. "Sometimes I wish I did. Come on inside and get off those wet shoes and socks. I'll dry them by the pot-bellied stove. How did you get here, anyway?"

"On a rope. You know, like Tarzan and Jane. It was fun, but I bogged down when I reached this side of the creek. If this is not where you live, why are you here?"

"Maybe I should ask you the same thing."

She told him about going for a walk, then chasing the puppy through the woods. "That's when I saw the rope. Want me to show you?"

"Oh, I know exactly where it is. When I was a kid, I dreamed of one day swinging from that rope. All the boys in the community would come here to swim, and they'd swing on it, but their goal was not to get to the other side, but to land in the creek."

"You didn't ever do it?"

"Nope. My mother wouldn't allow me to swim in the creek.

But after I grew up I'd come down here whenever I had things on my mind I needed to sort out. It's always been a place where I could shut out the rest of the world and think."

"That's what I want to do. Shut out the rest of the world."

"Hey, hey, what's with the tears? What's going on, Alexandra?"

She reached in her coat pocket and pulled out a folded, yellowed letter. "This."

"What is it?"

"It's a letter my mama gave Dabney before she died. Kiah's my daddy 'cause he raped my mama. Did you know that?"

Oliver swallowed hard. "Raped?"

"Yessir. It's in the letter."

"Do you understand the meaning of that word?"

"Sure. Josie said it's when a man don't really love a woman but he kisses her over and over and over anyway. And if you get kissed too many times, it means you're raped and then you can get . . . you know." She cupped her hand over her mouth and whispered, "PG!"

"Where did you get this letter?"

Her bottom lip poked out. "I found it."

"Do you mind if I read it?"

"I don't care."

Oliver unfolded the pages. His heart beat like a tom-tom as he read the words written by Zann to Dabney over ten years ago:

"My dearest Dabney,

250

My heart is heavy as I write this letter, but it's also filled with love and gratitude for what you were willing to do for me. I was wrong in allowing it, and I am so sorry. I thought I was doing it for Daddy, knowing it could hurt his ministry if people discovered I was pregnant, but deep down, I know I was doing it for my own prideful reasons." He stopped reading, pulled a handkerchief from his lapel and dabbed at his eyes.

"You crying, Oliver? What's wrong?"

"Nothing's wrong, kiddo. Everything is right." *So Dabney was telling the truth. She faked the birth. How she must hate me for doubting her.* He looked back down at the letter and silently read:

"I was embarrassed over the situation I found myself in and feared the stigma of being raped and the gossip which would surely follow. But to let you put yourself up for ridicule for my sake was selfish of me. You're the best friend I've ever had. The doctors won't tell me, but I know I'm dying. Mother and Daddy will be the guardians of my precious baby, but should anything ever happen to them, please promise me you'll keep up with Kiah's whereabouts, and take the child to him. I know if the time should ever come, he'll take good care of our baby.

All my love,

Zann"

Oliver blew out a heavy breath. "So that's why she did it."

Alex shrugged. "Did what?"

"I was just mumbling to myself. Alex, would you mind if I kept this letter for a while?"

"I dunno. What if Kiah finds out I took it and gets mad at me?"

"It isn't Kiah's letter. This belongs to Dabney. I promise you won't get into trouble. Trust me?"

"I reckon you're about the only person I do trust, Oliver."

He folded the letter and tucked it into his inside coat pocket. "I don't quite understand why you think Kiah was the one who . . . what I'm trying to say is—" Oliver had argued some difficult court cases in his day, but nothing had ever been as challenging as attempting to discuss such a sensitive subject with a ten-year-old.

"Raped my mama?" She finished his sentence without batting an eye.

Something about this scenario was backward. Shouldn't the kid be the one turning red, and not him, a twenty-seven-year-old man? "Uh, yes."

"It's right there in the letter. Last line. She says she was embarrassed she got raped. I would be too. Eeeyew! That's why I'm mad at Kiah. He was s'posed to wait until Mama was married and he kissed her anyway and that's just not right. Josie says it's a sin. Josie knows a lot about stuff like that. She's a year older than me."

"But where did you get the idea it was Kiah who . . . ?"

"She said in the letter that I'm their baby and he's my daddy."

"Are you sure?" He pulled the letter back out and unfolded it. His eyes skimmed over the last line . . . *he'll take good care of our baby.* He nodded. "I can see where this letter might seem a bit

252

confusing. One day, Dabney will sit down and explain everything to you, but for now, I need to get you back home before Kiah and Lizzie die from worry."

"But how will we get to the other side? I looked but I didn't see a rope on this side. You know where one is?"

Oliver laughed. Laughter came easy, now. Now that he knew the truth. "We don't have to cross the creek. This land, including this old shanty belongs to my family. There's a road on the other side of all the pine trees and a bridge that goes over the creek. My car's parked out on the road. You just can't see it from here because of the brush. Come on. I'll drive you back to Gladstone."

"Gee, thanks. I'm glad you've got a car. My hands have blisters from sliding on that rope." They walked out on the porch and just as he was about to walk down the steps, Alexandra threw her arms around his waist and squeezed. "I'm glad you were here, Oliver. I was really mad with Kiah and Lizzie when I left and I don't even know why. I reckon I was mad with ever'body. Ain't that crazy?"

"Not so crazy, sweetheart. But things are gonna get better. I promise." He scratched his head. Was he giving her false hopes? How could he be sure things would get better? A lot of minds would need swaying and in the end, someone was bound to be hurt. "Alexandra, did you tell Josie that Kiah, uh, you know . . . kissed your mama?"

"No way. You're the only person I've told."

"Good girl. Can we let our meeting this afternoon, our talks

253

and Dabney's letter be our secret? No one else should know. No one."

"Sure. I didn't wanna tell, nohow."

"Fine. I'll let you off near Gladstone. And kid, don't be too hard on Kiah and Lizzie. They love you very much, and so does Dabney."

"But I heard Lizzie tell Kiah that the only reason Dabney came to Goat Hill was to dump me off on him."

"Are you sure that was her exact words?"

"Well, I can't remember word-for-word, but that's what she meant."

"As I said, sweetheart, things aren't always as they seem. I surely got a lot of things wrong, but thanks to you, I see clearly now."

****

"But officer, I'm telling you, my boy has never stayed out this late. He's always very prompt. I demand that you send a posse out looking for him." Lula Weinberger clutched one hand over her heart and panted into the phone.

"Your boy? Excuse me, but I'll need your son's full name and the day he went missing."

"I only have one child, as you are well aware. Oliver Kipling Weinberger. I think he's been kidnapped, and the sooner you get a posse together, the better."

"A posse?"

"Yes. A posse. If you can't understand plain English, young

man, could you please hand the telephone over to someone who can?"

"I hear what you're saying, Mrs. Weinberger, but I'm afraid we can't do that."

"Of course, you can. And I'm not going to waste time on this phone arguing. Now, do as I say and issue a proclamation for every officer to scan the area."

"A proclamation?"

"Must you repeat my every word? Oliver knows dinner is served promptly at six o'clock every evening, and he is never late. Never. It's now eight o'clock and he still hasn't come home. Something dreadful has happened."

The officer chuckled in the phone.

"Are you laughing? Because if that was laughter I heard, trust me, I will report you to your superiors and you'll find yourself living the life of a hobo."

"Let me explain, ma'am. Number one: Your son is a grown man and has the right to miss supper if he so chooses."

"Dinner." She corrected. "And whether or not he has the right is not an issue. A mother knows her son, and Oliver would've called if he could've."

"Number two: We have no posse."

"Well, that's your problem, isn't it? Get one. Oliver could be tied up somewhere. I suppose there'll be a demand for a ransom. There are plenty of men in this town who can look for a missing person. Especially when it's a prominent attorney, like my son."

"Number three: I'm not sure how to go about issuing a proclamation as you suggested. Wouldn't it be just as effective if I looked across the desk and told Deputy Wooten to glance down the street and see if he sees Oliver? That would be notifying *every* officer."

"Your facetiousness will cost you your job, young man." And with that, she slammed down the telephone.

Not ready to face his Mother and Sallie Belle, Oliver drove back to the shanty after dropping Alexandra off at Gladstone. At the sound of thunder, he ran from the car through the heavy brush and barely had time to get inside before the bottom fell out of the dark clouds. He stretched out on the knotty cotton mattress on the old iron bed and listened to the soothing sound of rain pelting the tin roof.

At eight-fifteen, he awoke with a start, jumped up and grabbed his keys. The rain had stopped, but Oliver was aware the real storm was yet to come. "Mother will be furious with me for missing dinner." He heard Dabney's voice in his head, as clear as the day she said, "Oliver, we're gonna have a do-over and it's gonna be such fun. When you look in the mirror, I want you to see what I see—the strong, compassionate, handsome man that lurks beneath the surface. He's inside you. We just have to figure out how to bring him out. But changing the outside is only the beginning. You're the only one who can cut the apron strings, Oliver."

Oliver groaned, seeing Sallie Belle's car parked in front of his house. Hoping to avoid a confrontation, he drove around to the back door, slipped off his shoes and tiptoed through the butler's pantry, into the kitchen and was on the third stair when Sallie Belle squealed. "Lula, he's home. Oliver is home." His mother rushed into the room and with Sallie Belle hugging on one side and his Mother hugging on the other, he lost his balance and the three almost toppled off the stairs. "Excuse me ladies, but I've had a very long day and am exhausted. I simply wish to head upstairs, take a hot shower and go to bed. Good night."

Lula covered her trembling lips with her hand. "Oh, you poor boy. We were frantic. How did you escape?"

His brow knitted together. "Escape? From what, Mother?"

"The thugs who held you hostage, of course. Were you tortured? Where did they take you?" She held his face between her two hands. "Oh, my poor boy. You must've been terrified."

"Mother, I have no idea what you're referring to. You sound as if I was kidnapped."

"Are you saying you weren't?"

"Of course not."

She quickly lowered her arms and placed her hands on her hips. "Then where were you, Oliver?"

"I had some things on my mind, and I needed to think before coming home."

"Oliver that's not a satisfactory explanation. I demand you tell me where you've been?"

Sallie said, "I know why he's afraid to tell."

The corner of Oliver's lip curled. "Do you, now? Then suppose you share it with my mother."

"Lula, they wouldn't have released him if he hadn't paid a ransom, but then they threatened to kill him if he told."

Lula gasped. "Well, of course. Oh, bless your heart, precious. I hope you didn't have to pay them too much, but I suppose all that really matters now is that you're home safe and sound."

Oliver rolled his eyes. "You two should consider writing fiction. Now, excuse me, please, I'm going to retire."

Chapter Thirty-Four

Dabney could hardly understand Dave on the phone for the laughter. "I'm sorry. What did you say? Something about someone named Sallie? Sallie who? You say she's getting married? Am I supposed to know her?"

"I'm sorry. I can't stop laughing. It's hilarious. I'll be home in a minute and I'll tell you then. It'll be fun to see the look on your face when I tell you. You'll laugh, too."

Dabney tasted the beef stew and added a little more black pepper. She'd just pulled the cornbread from the oven when the front door opened.

"Honey, I'm home," Dave yelled out.

She rolled her eyes. "I know you're funning, Dave, but really, you should be careful how you tease. Suppose someone heard you. These houses are awfully close together. You know how people love to talk."

"So let them talk. Who cares?"

"I do. And that brings up something I'd planned to discuss tonight with you, but I might as well bring it up now. Dave, I'm very grateful that you'd give me this job and a place to live, but I need to begin looking for employment elsewhere."

"Don't be silly. I can give you more money. Is that it? You want more money? Not a problem. It's ridiculous for you to think of looking for a job. I enjoy the company. Since the ex left me, it's been too quiet around here." He cackled. "There was plenty of hollering going on as long as she was here, and I kinda miss the racket. There's no need for you to go anywhere else. I'm not here half the time, and it isn't costing me a thing for you to live here.

"But it could cost me."

"You think I'm gonna charge you rent? No way."

"I wasn't referring to it costing me money. But it may cost me my reputation, which has taken me years to build back."

"So that's what's got you worried. Well, that's an easy fix."

"What d'ya mean?"

"Hold on." Dave left the room, and returned to the kitchen holding a tiny box. He got down on one knee, and Dabney stopped stirring the stew and glared as he looked up into her eyes.

"Dabney Foxworthy, will you marry me?"

She sucked in a lungful of air and exhaled slowly. "Stop kidding, Dave."

He opened the tiny mother-of-pearl box, and Dabney's gaze locked on a gorgeous diamond ring.

He grinned. "Does this look like I'm kidding?"

She dried her hands on a dishrag, walked over to the table and sat down. "But why, Dave? You don't love me."

"So what's love got to do with it? I've argued more divorce cases for people who married because they swore they loved one another than I have for those who admitted they married for some other cockeyed reason. Trust me, sweetheart, love is way overrated."

Her stomach felt as if she'd swallowed a bag of marbles. She wasn't sure why, but for some unknown reason, she was disappointed that Dave admitted to not being in love with her. Even if she didn't love him. Somehow, getting a proposal from a man who bluntly confessed to not loving her made her feel cheap.

He reached for her hand. Perhaps she should've drawn it back. She wasn't even sure why she didn't, but as if in a daze, she watched as he slid the gorgeous ring on her finger.

She stared at it for several seconds, the muscles in her face twitching. Then in a low voice, she said, "Why, Dave? If not for love, why do you want to marry me?"

"The question you need to ask is not why, but why not? For starters, you're afraid of what people will say when they find out we're living under the same roof, and a ring will squelch the rumors. Naturally, if either of us decide to try something different, I happen to know a good lawyer who'll untie the knot." His cackling grated against Dabney's deepest nerve.

"Dave, I know you're doing this for me, and I appreciate that you'd go to such lengths for my sake. But I can't. It doesn't make

261

sense."

"Dabney, it makes perfect sense. I got the idea this morning when I went by the Court House and everyone was saying Fauntleroy Weinberger had—"

"Don't, Dave."

"Oh, so you've heard already? I suppose it's all over town by now."

"I don't know what you're talking about, but I wish you wouldn't call him Fauntleroy. That's not his name."

His brow creased. "You're not still pining over the milksop are you?"

"No." Her heart thumped faster. Not only had she lied to Dave, she was lying to herself.

"Well, I'm glad, because you just lost out, if you were hoping to become Mrs. Oliver Weinberger. Sallie Belle Sellers has done put the noose around his neck."

"Noose? I have no idea what you're saying." Her pulse raced. Did she really want to know?

"It's been a known fact for years that the Sellers have been trying to push their homely daughter off on Oliver, but even Oliver didn't want to go home to that face every night. But the buzz around the Court House is that he finally said 'yes'."

Dabney tried to swallow the pain. "I hope they're very happy. What's she like?"

"You've met his mother and Sallie Belle is a carbon copy. I've never seen two women who were more alike. And Fauntleroy . . .

262

I'm sorry. Meant to say Oliver. Oliver jumps when—"

Dabney twisted the ring around on her finger. "I don't want to talk about Oliver. My only interest is finding out how I can get custody of Alexandra."

"Well, we have a birth certificate that lists you as the mother and Kiah as the father. And if that were the only evidence submitted, the judge would be sure to award the kid to you. I'd argue the child has been with her mother—that would be you—all her life, and that the father—that would be Kiah—has never been in the picture, but now he decides he wants her after finding out his wife is barren."

She shook her head. "Not only is that a lie, it sounds cruel."

"You're a real softy. But child custody cases are never fun, Dabney. The one who fights the hardest or the smartest is the one to win. And to tell the truth, I hate losing a case—especially to Oliver Weinberger—so let me do my job. If you'd kept that letter you received from the kid's mother, instead of showing it to Kiah, we'd be home free. But since you don't know where it is, there's always the chance he kept it. And if he did, his lawyer will use it to prove you aren't the birth mother. He'll paint you as a single woman without a way to provide financially for the child's needs, and no place to call home. He'll argue that you've never held a job other than that of a housekeeper and you've always had to live in someone else's home." He let out a long sigh. "Keep looking for the letter. I'd feel much better if I knew it wasn't in Kiah's possession."

Dabney clasped her hands together. "Dave, that's not the only letter."

"What? You have another one?"

"No. But I wasn't the only one who received a letter. Zann wrote both Kiah and me."

Dave threw his head back and grimaced. "Are you serious? What does his say?"

"I don't know. I never read it." She'd held the tears as long as she could. "We may as well give up. Kiah and Lizzie are going to get Alex, aren't they?"

"Hey, dry the tears. You think I'll let Fauntleroy win this case? No way. Trust me. We'll get the word out that we're engaged and plan a spring wedding. You'll flaunt the ring and we'll go to the hearing, arm-in-arm and play the part of the crazy-in-love couple."

"But it'd be a lie, Dave."

"What's with you? Don't you want the kid?"

"You know I do."

"Well, this is the only way. We don't have to *tell* people we're in love. We'll simply gush over one another in their presence and let them form their own opinion. So even if Kiah produces a letter that shows you aren't the mother, by the time I get through with my deliberation, I'll have that judge squalling. You'll come across as a one-of-a-kind, compassionate friend who sacrificed her own reputation to save, not only a preacher's ministry, but also his daughter from a lifetime of humiliation. You'll be seen as a modern-day martyr. I'll explain that after the selfless act of pretending to be pregnant, you then gave up opportunities to get married and have a family of your own. And why would you do that, he'll ask? I'll explain it was to help a down-on-his-luck preacher who needed you to raise his little granddaughter. And now for ten years, you've changed every diaper sat up through countless sleepless nights nursing little Alexandra through childhood illnesses and dried every tear. I'll point out the child has known no other mother. How cruel it would be to separate the two of you." He beamed as if the case was won already. "Then I'll look at you like a love sick puppy and announce to the judge that you and I are planning to marry and that we want to provide a stable home for the child."

Dabney's pulse raced. *He'd do that for me?* So he didn't love her and she didn't love him—but how hard would it be to learn to love someone who'd go to such lengths to get Alex back? She'd be forever in his debt, and as such would do everything in her power to be a good wife. She glanced around the bungalow. It was small, but in an elite neighborhood. She thought of the slum she grew up in, in Rooster Run, and wanted more for Alexandra. Marrying Dave Whigham would allow her to have a good life.

"I'll do it, Dave."

"Do it?"

"You know. Marry you. Anytime, anywhere. Just name it."

"'At a girl. This case is as good as won."

She would've preferred a little glee over the acceptance of his proposal, but he'd done nothing to make her believe his motive was anything more than a marriage of convenience.

Dave said, "I'll get the license, and just before he issues his ruling, I'll ask the judge if he'll tie the knot, after the hearing. That way, he'll know we're serious about getting married, and it will naturally help to influence his decision."

Chapter Thirty-Five

Oliver carefully laid out his suit with padded shoulders and plain white dress shirt that he planned to wear to the custody hearing. After dressing, he parted his hair on the side, tossed his spectacles in the trash can and with his shoulders thrown back, he trekked down the stairs, skipping every other one.

Sallie Belle was in the kitchen with his mother, and dozens of Bridal magazines were strewn across the table. Sallie shrieked. "Good grief, Oliver Weinberger, where is the costume party? You look hideous." When she reached up to sweep his hair from the side to the center, he grabbed her hand.

"Get used to it, *dear.*" He said with a slur.

Lula groaned. "Oliver, I will not let you make a fool out of yourself in that silly garb. Sallie Belle is right. You look hideous. Get upstairs this instant and put on the suit I bought you last week. Comb your hair to the center part, put on your spectacles, and show the world you're the aristocratic gentleman you were raised to be."

"Sorry, Mother. This is who I am. Kip Weinberger, Pro Bono lawyer from Goose Hollow."

The two women exchanged glances and then simultaneously broke out in laughter. His mother shooed him away with her hand. "Stop fooling, you silly boy. You said you were to be at a hearing at nine o'clock and you've barely enough time to make it as it is. You've had your fun. Now run upstairs and get decent, then come back and have breakfast. It's already on the table in the dining room."

"Not hungry." Oliver walked over and poured him a cup of coffee. He blew into the steaming cup. "Sorry if you two don't approve, but this is who I am, like it or not. And, Mother, you can turn my office into a sewing room or whatever suits you. I won't be needing it. Tonight, I'll be moving my things out. I've always dreamed of taking pro bono cases, and I'm now going to live out my dream. I love you, Mother, but your little boy has finally grown up. It just took him longer to become a man than it does most."

His mother rolled her eyes. "This kind of nonsense is what comes when one associates with low-lifes. It's that girl, isn't it? You're doing it to please *her*. That . . . that maid. Oliver, get hold of your senses. She's nothing but trash."

"Mother, I'm doing it for me, but you don't know Dabney and for you to say such vicious things about her is shameful. She's the kindest person I've ever known."

Sallie Belle shrieked. "Oliver Weinberger, you can't be

serious. I will not marry a no-account lawyer, and that's exactly what you'll become if you insist on carrying out this silly notion. You won't be able to afford even the necessities of life, with the clients you'll attract. I won't have it."

"I was hoping you'd feel that way. Good day ladies."

When Oliver arrived at the Court House, Dave Whigham and Dabney were standing in the hall. Dabney appeared nervous and glared at the floor. Dave acknowledged his presence with a polite nod and extended his hand. "Good morning. I'm Dave Holloway. Have we met?"

Oliver grinned. "Is it that much of a change, Dave?"

"Oliver? Oliver Weinberger, is it really you? The voice is yours, but where did you send that stuff-shirt lawyer?"

"You mean Fauntleroy? I understand he passed on."

"Well, I like the look. What about you, Dabney?"

She lifted her eyes and nodded. "Nice." Her heart thumped hard against the walls of her chest. Never had she seen such a fine-looking man, and to think he'd been hiding inside gangly-looking Oliver Weinberger's body. A change of apparel, removing the wire-rimmed spectacles and a different hairstyle had played a large part in the drastic change, but it was the obvious self-confidence that breathed new life from Oliver into the jaw-dropping, handsome Kip Weinberger. Dabney dropped her gaze when he caught her staring, but she'd never noticed what gorgeous eyes and long, thick lashes were hiding behind those awful wire-rimmed spectacles. He stood tall and self-assured the way she imagined an Army General to stand, though she'd never met a real live Army General. The slumped shoulders were gone and he walked with an air of confidence. If she stayed one minute longer, she'd burst into tears. Shifting on her feet, she said, "Dave, I think it's about time. Would you please escort me inside and show me where to sit?"

Dabney's knees turned to mush, seeing Lizzie and Kiah sitting on the left side of the room. Not knowing whether it was proper to speak, she merely tipped her head and offered a nervous smile. She was glad Alexandra wasn't with them. Not that she wasn't eager to see her, but she wouldn't want little Alex to be put through the agony. She was such a tender-hearted child, Dabney could only imagine the trauma it would've caused, had she been allowed to sit through a heated hearing, listening to people she loved fight over her.

Dave took a seat beside her, leaned over and whispered. "Can you believe the change in Weinberger? I didn't even recognize him. Big change from Fauntleroy. I wonder what caused it? If you ask me, the ol' boy must be in love. What a change."

"Shh. He'll hear you." When a woman walked in and handed a paper to Lizzie, Dabney's pulse raced. *It's the nurse. Alex must be sick.* Seeing Lizzie hesitate to open the envelope, Dabney's fears were confirmed. *Something's terribly wrong.* She watched as Lizzie read the contents, then buried her head in sobs. Or was she laughing? It was hard to tell. Dabney kept glancing their way, but concluded whatever was in that envelope appeared to be good.

Kiah said, "Wasn't that the doc's nurse? What's going on, honey? If it's Alexandra, go take care of her. It isn't necessary that you be here."

"It's not Alex."

"Then what?"

"There's going to be a funeral."

"What? A funeral? Whose? What are you talking about?"

Lizzie giggled. "The rabbit died."

"Lizzie, are you alright? We don't have a—" His words caught in his throat. "Wait a minute. You aren't saying what I think you're saying."

She nodded emphatically. "Yes. Yes. Yes. The test results just came back. Sad a little bunny has to die for a woman to have pregnancy results verified. I didn't want to tell you, darling, because I was afraid it wasn't true. But those mornings I was throwing up, when you contributed it to nerves, was actually the smell of bacon frying. Kiah, we're gonna have a baby. Can you believe it? A baby."

He reached over and grabbed her in his arms and they cried happy tears together.

"So when did you begin to suspect it?"

"The morning after we had the long talk and I told you that as much as I loved Alexandra, I had to let her go. I was being selfish to want to bribe her into staying with us, when I knew in my heart she and Dabney belonged together. The next morning I threw up for the first time, and I can't tell you how I knew, but I knew with that first heave that I was pregnant. And I know that I'll carry this baby to term."

"Honey, I pray you're right, but—"

"There are no 'buts,' Kiah. I can't explain, but I have full assurance that God gave me this miracle the minute I let go of Alexandra. I still don't know why we had to put Dabney through the ordeal of this hearing. Why couldn't we have just told her our decision and save her from the torment?"

"We could have. But after talking with Oliver, he felt it would be better to go through the motions, and after all, he's the attorney." He glanced up at a large clock on the wall. "It's past time to begin. I wish the judge would come on and get this over with. Poor Dabney looks like a ghost. I'm almost tempted to go over there and tell her."

Dabney continued to keep her gaze focused on the strange goings-on, on the other side of the room. Then it hit her. *They know. Why else would they be looking as if they've won a million dollars? The hearing hasn't even begun, yet they know already they're going to be awarded custody.*

She braced and silently vowed to be strong when the judge entered the chambers. Oliver spoke with the judge privately, then Dave was called to the bench and the three whispered for what seemed like an eternity. When Oliver slapped Dave on the back and laughed, chills went down Dabney's spine. She'd never attended a custody hearing, but this wasn't going the way she'd imagined. What could be so funny? Had Dave sold her out? Maybe he didn't want the responsibility of raising a child and agreed to let Oliver win. That was it, wasn't it? Whatever made her think she could trust lawyers?

She slowly relaxed as she listened to Dave present his case, just as he'd rehearsed it. He was very eloquent in his presentation, though it was a bit more dramatic than Dabney felt necessary. Had she been wrong in assuming it was over before it began? She let out a hearty breath of air, realizing she'd allowed unsubstantiated fears to inflate into unfounded allegations. Dave was doing a super job in his deliberations. But Dabney flinched, when in his final remarks, Dave said, "Judge, Miss Foxworthy and I would be ever so grateful if you'd perform a marriage ceremony at the conclusion of this hearing. I have the license in hand, and we're eager to become Mr. and Mrs. David P. Whigham."

Dabney bit her trembling lip. She couldn't deny she was grateful for Dave's willingness to marry her in order to assure she'd get Alexandra. But what was in it for him? Did beating Oliver in a court hearing mean so much to him that he'd take such a drastic measure? Was marriage so meaningless that he'd jump in and jump out of it as carelessly as if it were as simple as crawling in and out of bed?

Why question Dave's sanity, when her own was up for question. By agreeing to marry him, it was true she'd have the financial support needed to raise Alex, but the child had already been through an emotional upheaval. Was it really fair to bring her into a home void of love? Dabney didn't want to admit it, but it was clear that Kiah and Lizzie could offer a loving environment. They'd be excellent parents. Alex could have it all if she remained with the Graves. As hard as she tried, accepting the truth was a bitter pill to swallow.

When the judge issued his verdict and gave Dabney custody, she broke out in uncontrollable sobs. Dave took her hand and squeezed. "Come on, we need to hurry, sweetheart. The judge has agreed to perform the ceremony, but he has to leave in fifteen minutes."

Dabney's knees knocked as she and Dave hurried to the front of the room and stood before the black-robed man. The judge read the vows from a book, then said, "If there's anyone who can show just cause why this man shouldn't be joined to this woman, let them speak now or forever hold their peace."

A voice from the back, boomed. "I object to this marriage, your honor."

Dabney jerked her head around to see Oliver rushing toward the bench. "Kip?"

The judge cleared his throat, then boomed. "On what grounds, young man?"

"On the grounds that I love this woman and she loves me."

The lines on the judge's face softened, and he tapped his fist to his lips, appearing to hide a peculiar smile. "Is that so, Miss

Foxworthy? Are you in love with Oliver Weinberger?"

She glanced at Oliver, then at Dave. *What's going on? Why were they both grinning, as if they were in cahoots?*

The judge said, "Miss Foxworthy? Would you be so kind as to answer my question? Do you, or do you not love Oliver Weinberger?"

She pulled at the neck of her sweater, and glanced back at Dave. "Yessir. Yessir, I reckon it's so."

"Then according to the law vested in me . . . I refuse to perform this ceremony."

Oliver waved a paper in the air. "Pardon me, your honor, but I have a license here, and as soon as I get my beloved's signature on the bottom line, if the bride doesn't object, we still have nine minutes left before you have to leave. I believe that'll be sufficient time for you to tie the knot."

"Do you have witnesses?"

"Yes, he does!" Kiah and Lizzie ran arm-in-arm to the front.

Lizzie hugged Dabney. "Congratulations, Dabney. Alex is where she needs to be. You're her Mother. Her *real* Mother. I hope you and Oliver will allow her to have a relationship with us. We'd love to be her Aunt Lizzie and Uncle Kiah. I've always wanted to be an aunt. That sweet little girl has stolen our hearts. You've done an amazing job raising her."

"Thank you, Lizzie. I have a funny feeling you knew the outcome of this hearing, even before we began. I know how desperately you want a child, so why would you give up?"

275

"God showed me it was the right thing to do, Dabney. When I told Kiah I couldn't go through with it, he called Oliver, who contacted the judge over a week ago. I understand that when Dave talked to Oliver, he discovered the tide was turning. Not only were you in love with Oliver, but that Oliver was in love with you. Dave suggested Oliver apply for a marriage license and bring it with him to the courtroom."

"Are you serious? Dave was the instigator?"

"Yes, but I can't tell if you're happy or sad. I see the tears, yet you're smiling."

"They're grateful tears, Lizzie. People misunderstand Dave and often only see the rough edges, but a wise old man once told me there's a little bad in the best of us and a little good in the worst of us. I believe it. There's more than just a little good in Dave Whigham. There's an abundance of good. He has a heart of gold. The man doesn't love me, but I have no doubt he would've married me, anyway, if it were the only way for me to win custody of Alexandra."

Lizzie raised a brow. "Oh, but I think Dave loves you more than you know. He loved you too much to let you marry the wrong man."

Kiah nudged Lizzie and nodded toward the bench.

The judge pulled a fob watch from his coat pocket. "Would someone *please* hand the lady a pen, before I miss my train?"